Ruby TUESDAY

DEBBIE CHASE

World Castle Publishing, LLC
Pensacola, Florida
Copyright © Debbie Chase 2021
Paperback ISBN: 9781955086592
eBook ISBN: 9781955086608
First Edition World Castle Publishing, LLC, August 16, 2021
http://www.worldcastlepublishing.com

Cover: Karen Fuller
Editor: Maxine Bringenberg

Chapter One

"Just back off for me, will you? Please?" asked Rose. "I'll never get the job if you're applying for it as well." She must have noticed the mutinous look on my face because she said pleadingly, "Please, Ruby...."

I shook my head. "I can't, Rose...I really want this job. I've always wanted to work in the school library, and this is just too good an opportunity to miss." I glanced at her from the corner of my eye. At her pretty face, light blue eyes framed with long black lashes set above high cheekbones, the lips shaped like a fancy bow on a gift, the lower one being as thick and fleshy as a seductive pout. A face that I gazed at every day. Oh, not Rose's face, but my own, barely noticing it, really, though. Rose's face was my mirror. Rose was my identical twin.

We were in our hometown, Emsworth in Hampshire, sitting on the harbor wall, our legs, long and tanned, dangling down. A wrinkly expanse of sand spread with rock pools and seaweed sparkled in the sunshine, and boats, lopsided and abandoned, patiently waited for the tide. People carrying buckets and spades were digging deep, searching for seafood for tea, and kids with massive nets were trying to catch scuttling crabs.

Seagulls squawked overhead, one flying low enough to try to steal the sandwich from Rose's hand. Horrified, she batted it away and ducked her head as it gave a ghostly squeal and fluttered into the clouds. The sun, hot and yellow as a bowl of custard, scudded across the sky, pushed by a salty breeze. It was almost June, and we had the whole summer ahead of us. And today was Saturday, which was even better.

"Who's to say you'd get the job anyway?" I asked her, taking a bite of my own food and attracting unwanted attention from a mass of meaty gulls that hovered nearby. "Maybe neither of us will get it."

"You've already got your foot in the door," she whined. "You've got a far better chance than me."

What she meant was that I already worked in the school, a secondary school in Warblington, at the reception desk. I enjoyed my job. I loved greeting visitors, liaising with teachers and parents, talking with the kids and telling them off when they ran along the corridors or pushed and jostled on the stairs. I got on well with my colleague, Jo, who was super-efficient, smooth and in control. I'd done okay exam-wise at school, then gone to college to do a computer course. In between, I'd passed my driving test, which I was really proud of. But the downside—do you know how expensive it is to buy and run a car?

Rose hadn't done too well at school and had drifted

from one low-paying job to another before going to college to re-sit her failed exams, while I'd gone on ahead and gotten a job. A job that I could hardly believe was mine at the tender age of nineteen in a school, with all the benefits it entailed, including the holidays. But now, three years later, Rose, successful exam results tucked firmly under her belt, wanted a good job in a school, which just happened to be the job I wanted too. Surely there were other jobs in other schools? You'd think there would be, wouldn't you?

I knew that the two of us needed the money — after all, we were trying to save for a deposit on our own place. Being happy at home with Mum and Dad came second to our need for independence, and buying somewhere together was the only way we could afford to do it.

"Will you think about it, Ruby?" she asked, swallowing the last morsel of sandwich and, crumpling the wrapper in her hand, slid down from the harbor wall and placed it in the nearby bin.

Reluctantly, I nodded as we began to walk back down the High Street towards home, past the little gift shops, charity shops and cafes, Mum's workplace as a PA, the solicitors "Butcher & Steele," and the two most popular pubs in Emsworth — the rough wooden seats outside already taken on such a warm day — the Bluebell and the Coal Exchange. We attracted a lot of stares from strangers as usual, with our identical looks and clothes, but friendly nods and waves from the locals.

I always tried to dress in private, which was difficult when I shared a room — even a room with a divider decorated with fancy butterflies and flowers set square down the middle — so I could at least be different from Rose. But as if by magic, she always seemed to know what I would be wearing that day. Ha, I suspected that she had some sort of physic powers. Today we wore matching denim shorts and T-shirts with trainers.

"Do you spy on me when I'm dressing?" I asked her repeatedly, only for her to vehemently deny it. Today, like a couple of gypsies, we wore large silver hoop earrings. Now how could she possibly have known that without watching me?

In fact, the only distinguishing mark between us was the large mole I had on the left of my nose. "Thank God for that mole," Mum always said, "It was the only way me and your dad could tell the two of you apart when you were babies."

Of course, I'd been teased unmercifully by our so-called "friends" at school. "Oh, you mean Ruby with the mole that lives in the hole?" I remembered Leanne saying in a sing-song voice, and Claire took great pleasure in calling me Simon Templar because the hero from an old program in the seventies had a mole just like mine. Mum and Dad laughed at that a lot.

"Look," said Claire, showing them a picture on her phone. "I think he's called Roger Moore."

"Yes," agreed Dad. "He was Simon Templar, and the program was called *The Saint*. One of my favorites."

"When you're an old lady," Rose said one sunny day as we played in the garden, "You'll have long spiky hairs growing from your mole, like a wicked witch." That comment made me cry, and I ran to Mum in a frenzy, tears pouring down my cheeks.

"You won't say anything about the job to Mum and Dad, will you?" whispered Rose, bringing me out of my reverie, as we walked up the garden path and entered the house through the wide-open back door. There was a lovely smell of cooking, and Mum, May Deacon—named for the month she was born—turned from the stove and smiled, telling us that tea wouldn't be too long.

"We've just had a snack," I told her. "So we can wait."

She frowned, and I suspected was just about to tell us off for eating so soon before tea but changed her mind and said, "How's Emsworth on this fine sunny day?" She peered over her shoulder and fixed us with her dark brown gaze, so unlike mine and Rose's light blue eyes. Without a doubt, we inherited them from our dad, Doctor Stan Deacon, who was at work as we spoke in his small GP practice—just three partners—in nearby Havant. Our dark hair definitely came from Mum, though.

"Crazy busy as usual," we said in unison.

"I'll call you when it's ready," she replied, "When Dad's home."

"Well?" asked Rose as we climbed the stairs to our room. "You won't, will you?"

"No, I won't say anything to anyone," I whispered back. "But I need time to think, Rose. I'm really interested in this job."

Sitting down on my neat and tidy bed, I noticed that Rose's side of the room was a mess, as usual. Piles of books littered the floor, along with screwed-up tissues and empty chocolate wrappers—even though she said she was always watching her weight. It drove me mad!

I went to the window and, opening it wider, looked out on the garden that was bursting with colorful flowers. Bees buzzed amongst their silky soft petals, collecting nectar for the yummy honey that I drizzled over my breakfast every morning. The lawn looked ragged, the grass being slightly too long and needing mowing, which I was sure would be Dad's first job when he got in from work. Yeah, even before he sat down to eat, which was just as well, as the sandwich I'd eaten earlier lay heavy as a stone in my full stomach.

Throwing myself back down on my bed, I wished for the hundredth time that I had a room of my own. But as we lived in a two-bedroom house, there was no chance of that any time soon. Okay, this house was small, but as it was in Emsworth and overlooking the harbor, it was much sought after. Mum and Dad had lived in it for years, even before we were born, when the whole row of two up, two downs were nondescript, tumbledown, even considered poor dwellings. But they'd done right to buy it, as it was now worth more than double the original price.

The smell of salt from the sea wafted through the window, and something else too, so I wrinkled my nose. Mud, streaming in on the breeze from Langstone. Langstone on the mud. We'd had fun there as kids, squelching in the slimy stuff like basking hippos, plastic shoes on our feet, or sitting with our cousins in an old discarded fishing boat, screaming as crabs scuttled around in the water, and slimy seaweed long as a mermaid's hair tangled around our legs.

"Have you got a text from Vanessa?" asked Rose, interrupting my nostalgic thoughts.

Scrabbling in my bag for my phone, I went to messages. "Yeah, meet tonight in the Coal Exchange? No, I don't think I'll go. Not in the mood."

Rose's face peered, frowning, over the top of the divider. "Why?"

I shrugged. "Just as I said, not in the mood." I knew it would be the same old, same old. Same old group of people. Same old pubs and places. And as well as that, even though I loved my sister, did I have to go everywhere with her? I'd tried getting involved with separate groups of people who had interests that I had, like writing and art, but Rose always followed me, turning up unannounced and, being the more forceful personality, like an eclipse of the sun, she soon put me firmly in the shade. I didn't think she meant to do it, but it always seemed to happen.

"James will be there," she said cheekily. "He really likes you, Ruby…." She paused for a minute and then said, "Don't you think it's weird that he likes *you* so much when we look so alike?"

"What do you mean?"

"Well, why can't he settle for me? What's the difference?"

"Rose, "I said indignantly, "It's not just looks. We have our own personalities, of course." And then, as an afterthought, although genuinely wanting to know, I asked, "Would you like James to take an interest in you?"

"No, I don't think so," she replied, "Although he is pretty cute but too tall for me, I think my neck would suffer eventually — and anyway, I like shorter, stockier men. But anyway, what's the use, it's you he likes? I think he's turned on by your mole."

I smiled and shook my head. God, that mole! I'd thought so many times of having it removed, but how would people tell us apart if I did?

My thoughts turned to James. James Lister. We'd known him and his sister, Lara, since school. He lived nearby, only a couple of streets away, and worked in an engineering firm in Emsworth called Sonic, on the aptly named Seagull Lane.

As Rose had said, he was cute and very tall, so much so that I always had to crane my neck to look up into his face. A face that lit up like a switched-on light bulb every time he smiled. With deep brown eyes and long, long lashes, all of this was framed with shoulder-length black hair and a fringe that often grew too long. He was always — nervously it seemed, especially when I was around — pushing it out of the way with his fingers.

I knew he liked me, but I was restless lately and needed a change, and becoming romantically involved with a local boy was perhaps not what should be happening at the moment. Maybe it was a good thing Rose wanted me to "back off," as she'd said, from applying for the library job. Maybe I should leave the school altogether and go travelling.

A sudden idea came to me, exploding in my head like a firecracker, and I thought, *But I wouldn't have to leave the school. The six-week summer holidays are coming up very soon. Instead of staying local with Rose and going on days out to places like Southsea, Hayling Island, and the Witterings, or even Prinstead, why don't I go off alone to…? I don't know.* Several countries raced through my mind before I came to the obvious one, the nearest one, one that was easy to get to from Portsmouth, *France*! Excitement gripped me, and my heart started beating really fast as if I'd been exercising hard with one of those kettlebell things. *I could get a ferry from Portsmouth to either Caen or St. Malo. St. Malo would probably be best. I've always wanted to go there, and now this is my chance.*

I glanced at the room divider, imagining Rose lounging on her bed on the other side, nonchalantly scrolling through her phone, head bent, staring at the screen, and making plans for tonight. Thinking about what she was going to wear, wondering what boys would be there. I knew she quite fancied James's friend, Steve, and would probably home in on him just to brighten up the evening a bit while I was planning a holiday miles away from here. What would she say? I knew without a doubt that she would be mad, that she would try to stop me. She wouldn't be able to go with me because of a lack of funds, so I would have to keep it a secret. My own little secret.

While she was out tonight, I would google ferry crossings, work out costs and travel dates, and look at accommodations in St. Malo. Yes! A big grin split my features until I felt sure I looked just like one of those yellow smiley face patches that Mum painstakingly sewed on her jeans in the nineteen seventies.

Feeling eyes boring into me, I glanced up to see Rose once again peering over the divider.

"What are you grinning at, Ruby Tuesday? You look like the cat that got the cream."

"Maybe I have," I said teasingly, feeling buoyed up with the excitement of my big secret.

Hearing the whirring of the mower, I jumped up again and peered from the window to see Dad, still wearing his suit trousers, shirt sleeves rolled up, trundling backwards and forwards, leaving smooth cut grass in his wake. Our dad, who in his mid-fifties looked at least ten years younger, and with his piercing blue eyes and razored greying hair, bore the nickname at his little GP practice of "Silver Fox."

"Dad's obsessed with that lawn," said Rose lazily, coming to stand at my side. She stood quietly for a few minutes before saying, "James will be sure to ask about you tonight. As I said before, he really likes you. Do you think he stands any chance at all?"

I glanced at her and said, "No, not at the moment. I don't want a local boy. I—" Mum's shout up the stairs telling us to come down for tea interrupted our conversation, although I just had a few seconds to change the subject and say, "I won't stand in your way, Rose. I'll back off from the library job as you asked me to."

Surprise opening her blue eyes wide, Rose replied, "Oh wow, Ruby, thank you."

"It doesn't mean you'll get it, though, Rose. Other people in the school, far more qualified people, are interested in it too, you know."

She nodded and squeezed my hand in another thank you as we left the room and sped down the stairs to the dining room. Thoughts whirred around in my head like clothes in a washing machine. An ugly green imp suddenly appeared on my shoulder, whispering in my ear. *What have you done giving up on applying for the job so easily? You wanted that job — it could have been yours.*

Be strong, I thought as I turned my head, and with difficulty, glared at the ugly green imp, thinking, *Yes, but I might not get it anyway*, and *I need an adventure before I turn old and sour. France beckons.*

"You okay, Ruby?" asked Rose, giving me an odd look as we took our seats and gazed around at the dishes that stood on the table, steaming dishes full of vegetables and potatoes and the pièce de résistance, Mum's special chicken casserole.

I nodded my head. "Of course I am."

"Ha," said Dad happily, clapping his hands together, a smile creasing his face. "My girls, my double the trouble. What adventures have you been up to today?"

Double the trouble. The tale of Dad at our birth was legendary and had been told many times at family gatherings.

It always went like this, with Dad holding a captive audience right in the palm of his hand. "Right in front of my startled eyes, the first one, Ruby, popped out." He'd look around at the audience then, blue eyes glittering, and say, "I knew it was Ruby because of the mole." This always got a good round of laughter. "And, after peering closely and shaking my head, I said, 'Hmm, a girl. One is trouble….' And then the second one, Rose, slipped out and, peering closely at this one too and shaking my head again, I said, 'Hmm, another girl. And two is double the trouble.'"

Of course, as Rose had been born second, she'd always been known as the afterbirth, the placenta—which, not at all amusing to her, made me smile every time. And then, of course, there were our names. I was Ruby Tuesday because Mum and Dad had always been really big fans of the Rolling Stones. And Rose was Rose Marie because of their love of country music! "That's not the only reason," Mum always told us. "You were both so precious to us. And a ruby is a precious jewel, and a rose a precious flower."

"Well?" asked Dad, as Mum encouraged us to take plenty of vegetables. "Adventures? Come on, girls, let's hear about your escapades today."

I had to grin at Dad's word "adventures" — very apt. Excitement rose high up in my chest and into my throat, just like Christmas morning, as my impending secret adventure came to mind. Rose gave me a look that clearly said, "Don't you dare tell them about the library job." We began to tell him about our day while helping ourselves to the plentiful good food.

Chapter Two

Mum and Dad had met young, very young, at school. Dad always said there was never anybody else for him and that it was love at first sight. "Even that awful maroon and grey school uniform and knee-high socks that were always pooling around her ankles didn't put me off," he always said with a laugh. I never heard Mum say the same, but God, she must love him—after all, she'd stayed with him for years. They had a lot of history, the most important thing, of course, being Rose and me—"The best thing that ever happened to us," they always said—although we didn't appear until they were well into their thirties.

They still spent all their evenings and weekends together, walking the local beauty spots and frequenting the nearby pubs and restaurants. Both loved the garden, Mum dead heading and planting while Dad mowed the lawn and carried out repairs, and then Mum did her own thing at the health center like yoga, Pilates, and swimming, and Dad played golf.

Mum had been born in Emsworth, in a very small hospital called Northlands, a lovely old house situated near the station, which was long gone — "Demolished years ago," Mum had told us. Dad was born in the beautiful city of Chichester, which was where Grandma and Grandad — Dad's mum and dad — used to live. Both died when we were young, whereas Nan and Grandad, Mum's mum and dad, still alive and kicking, lived in Havant in a lovely house on West Street called Westfield House.

Rose and I used to love staying there when we were little. We were let loose to explore the whole house, silently creeping through the dark rooms, often finding Nan chatting in her "telephone room," as she always called it, or with Grandad in the sitting room, fire blazing, shouting at the wrestling on a Saturday afternoon. We loved the old musty attic, still with the bells on the wall for summoning the servants many years before, and the bright, airy conservatory, where we enjoyed the family parties. The house was huge, but then so was the family, consisting of lots of aunties and uncles and cousins, and second cousins, and probably third and fourth cousins as well. For all I knew, I could walk past a member of the family on Emsworth High Street every day and not even know who they were.

A pitter-patter of wet drops on my bare arms and the top of my head brought me back to earth, and, glancing up, I found that the sun had disappeared behind massed dark clouds that looked fit to burst at any minute. Oh no, it had been sunny when I set off for home.

Jesus is washing his floor, I thought as I dashed to stand beneath the protective leafy canopy of a tree, one of many lining the paths on my walk home from Warblington School to Emsworth. What on earth made me think that, Jesus is washing his floor?

It put me in mind of a story Mum told me about something I'd asked her when I was little. Apparently, I'd said very seriously, "Does Jesus smack dicky bird's legs?"

"What did you say to that?" I asked as I shook my head and giggled at my stupid young self.

"I told you that no, Jesus would never do that," Mum replied, "And that he loves all animals and birds." Wow, I must have been a strange child.

Hoisting my rucksack higher on my back, I carried on walking. Being a bit of a fitness freak, I always walked home from school. It was only a couple of miles each way, but hey, four miles a day could do a body a lot of good. Rose, needless to say, thought I'd lost my mind. She'd always been one of the girls at school who forged notes from their mum on PE day, especially when it was cross country or hockey. Whereas I had been there at the head of the queue, ready and raring to go.

Typical, I thought. *The last day of the summer term, six whole weeks of freedom stretching ahead, and of course, it's raining in sheets.*

Pulling a rain slicker from my rucksack, I put it on and pulled the hood up over my dark hair. I stood for a few minutes watching the rain drops as they hammered into the ground like tiny silver bullets. People scurried past, eager to get home, and traffic thundered by, sending out a fine spray like somebody sneezing. Quickly, my boots squelching through the puddles, I walked on, the rain easing off to a silvery haze. As I reached Emsworth town center, the sun came out from behind the clouds, glimmering in patches of blue, and the rain finally stopped, so I lowered my hood and shook my hair back from my face.

People came tentatively out of swinging pub doors, taking cursory glances up at the sky and, after giving the benches a hasty wipe, sat down with a weary sigh to sip their tea time beers and wines. Cooking smells wafted lazily along the street, and families sat on benches eating fish and chips, besieged by clouds of greedy honking seagulls. Colorful boats bobbed up and down on the rippling sea. A runner streaked by, soaked from head to toe, slipping and sliding on the wet cobbles, and a black and white border collie bounded along, gazing up at its owner, its tail wagging in excitement.

"Hey, Ruby." A figure loomed in front of me, a figure so tall I had to crane my neck to look up at him. A smile lit up his face like a megawatt light bulb, and his deep brown eyes twinkled. Stubble layered his chin and cheeks, which I had to admit looked really cool and attractive.

"Hi, James, how are you?" The fleeting thought — *oh my God — what must I look like* went through my mind. I had visions of stringy damp hair and a rain-soaked sweaty — hopefully, it was more dewy? — looking face, and added to that the really unfashionable rain slicker. It wasn't my best look.

"Yeah, I'm good. You, Ruby?" I nodded as he frowned and said, "I haven't seen you for ages. Not with the usual crowd or even with Rose, which is pretty weird. You two are usually me and my shadow." He laughed, showing his lovely white teeth.

"Well, Rose and I can't be together constantly. Both of us at any one time is really too much of a good thing."

He smiled and said, "Did you get caught in the rain?"

Which put me in mind of a song that Mum loved, something about walking in the rain with the one I love. The big guy? Barry White?

"Yeah, it came down pretty heavy earlier, but it's great now. Look at the sun." We both gazed up at the sky where that great yellow globe hung like a cardboard cut-out hastily colored bright yellow by a child. James nodded, and we grinned at each other as awkwardly, shyly, he looked down at the ground and then back at me, and just stared until I said, "Oh well, better head home. See you, James."

"Yeah, yeah, see you, Ruby. It's been good to chat."

I began to walk away, almost tripping over a dog's lead that was stretched tightly across the path. The owner was gazing without a care in the world into Diamond & Dewers, the Butcher's shop window, contemplating the price of sausages or chicken legs, no doubt, instead of keeping a vigilant eye on the whereabouts of his dog's lead.

"Oh, sorry, love," he said, a small, portly man with a droopy mustache, as he saw me stumble and quickly jerked the lead away. A strong hand gripped my arm, and I looked up once again at James.

"Oh…thank you," I said, "You saved my life." I giggled nervously.

"That's okay, and yeah, dog owners should watch out for that. It happens all the time." He gave the portly man a bit of a look before blurting out, "Look, Ruby, I need to ask you something."

I had a feeling he was going to ask me out, and I wasn't sure what to say. I couldn't tell him I was sneaking away the very next day on an adventure. I was tempted to confide in him, but no, I couldn't take the risk. Not even Mum and Dad knew I was going off alone.

Very hot and flustered by now, he said, "Look…. Can I…? Ruby…will you go out for a drink with me? Just the two of us? Sometime soon? Well, this weekend, if you're not busy."

"James, I—"

But before I could say anything else, he stammered, "It's okay. You've probably got somebody else anyway. You're so pretty and outgoing, and…interesting, why would you want to see me?" He turned his head away, pretending to look at the crowds of people walking along the High Street, his hands dug deep into his pockets. People jostled around us, taking interested sneaky glances, trying to listen to our conversation.

"No, James, it's not that. There's nobody else." In so many ways, I wanted to say, "Can you wait until I come back from France?" But instead, I blurted out, "I just don't want a boyfriend at the moment, or even a casual friend, really." And then I said a really lame thing. "I'm finding myself, I suppose…."

"Yeah, I understand. It's okay. Um…I'll see you around then, Ruby."

"Thanks, James, for helping me earlier. I'd have looked a fool if I'd fallen."

He gave a small smile, his lips turning up slightly at the corners, and said, "If you ever change your mind, this is my number. Make sure you put it in your phone."

He pressed a scrap of paper into my hand and, leaning forward, gently kissed my mouth right at the very edge of my lower lip. A sharp pain like an arrow pierced my chest, and I felt breathless and weak as if my bones had turned to mush. Clutching the piece of paper in my hand, I put my fingers to the place he'd kissed, feeling the warmth of it and wondering if the pain in my heart was a feeling of regret.

~*~

Arriving home, I walked through the open front door and into the hallway. I breathed in a strong smell of cooking, something hot and spicy that seeped like a dense fog between the cracks of the closed kitchen door. It looked as though Mum's special chicken curry was on the menu tonight. I was glad there was nobody about and wanted to get to the privacy of my side of the room, so to speak, first of all, to rid myself of my damp clothes, and then to sit and really think about that truly romantic moment that had just taken place on the High Street between myself and James.

I kept reminding myself that this was the same James I'd known since school, the same James I'd thought of as a brother, really, that I'd refused to go out with many times before — albeit only asked on a casual basis and not a proper date — and that I'd thought of as a friend.

How come one meeting with him out of the blue, when I was just going off alone on the adventure of a lifetime, had suddenly given me the collywobbles? I'd found myself even admiring his stubble, for God's sake! And what was even worse was that he'd given me his number, so unless I got rid of that piece of paper right now and put it firmly in the bin, I would be able to text or ring him at any time, even when I was away. Tempting or what?

Stopping me in my tracks, Rose's voice came loud and clear from behind the kitchen door. "Well, Mum, you're now looking at the new library assistant at Warblington School. I start after the summer holidays."

There was a short silence before Mum said, "What are you talking about, Rose? That's Ruby's job, surely."

"She didn't want to apply," said Rose confidently. "She gave me a total free rein and said she had no interest in the job. She really likes being on reception and didn't want to give it up."

The sound of the kettle coming to a bubbling boil drowned out some of the conversation, then I heard Mum say, "Hmm. I'm a bit puzzled as to why Ruby made that choice. She was so keen on the library job."

"Well, you know what she's like, very changeable."

I frowned at that comment. Rose knew I wasn't changeable, that I had really seriously wanted the library job. But then again, she was right. I had backed off and given her free rein, but only because I had itchy feet and, to be truthful, because of the competition for the job, I hadn't expected Rose to get it. People who were far more qualified than her had said they were going to apply. Maybe they hadn't. Rose hadn't even told me when the interviews were taking place, trying to shield me from any upset, I suppose, seeing as how she knew how much I was giving up.

Well, whatever, I thought, as I ran quickly upstairs to our room. It was too late now. I'd have to grin and bear it. Thank God I was going off on holiday and could at least get away from it all. It would have been too difficult to hide my disappointed face from Mum, that's for sure.

Before Rose came upstairs, I quickly pulled my rucksack from underneath the bed and began to fill it with clothes. Shorts and T-shirts, underwear, a pair of jeans, a swimming costume, flip flops, and a sundress. I was going to travel extremely light. I dithered with the trusty rain slicker before deciding to take it in case of bad weather.

My plan was to wake at the crack of dawn and somehow sneak past a sleeping Rose. Hopefully, she would go out tonight, have a few drinks, and be out for the count. I was going to stash my bag in the garden shed and pick it up on my way out. Dad didn't always check that it was locked — and anyway, I knew where he kept the key.

I felt a bit guilty at going off without saying a word to Mum and Dad, but it was the only way. If Rose knew, she would surely follow me, and I didn't want that at the moment. I needed to get away, not only because of Rose having gotten the library job, but also because of James, and more importantly, because I wanted to experience life without a twin. Without my other half, the other side of my face. In fact, what it was like to be me and only me, Ruby Tuesday Deacon.

Chapter Three

The city of Portsmouth receded into the distance, looking more and more like a toy town, its buildings, houses and shops becoming smaller and smaller and then slowly disappearing, as the ferry chugged further and further out to sea, bobbing up and down on the choppy waves, all the way to St Malo. I smiled to myself, thinking about happy times with Mum, Dad, and Rose when we'd sailed to the Isle of Wight for our summer holidays. Seagulls wheeled and squawked overhead. Would I ever get away from the pesky things? They were bad enough in Emsworth, but here, out in the proper deep sea as it were, they were even worse, like white phantoms in the sky, their plaintive cries sending shivers running down my spine.

Gripping the deck rail hard with cold hands, I smiled with excitement and even awe, pleased with myself, happy that I'd gotten this far. A strong cool wind ruffled my hair, and people milled about, pushing and jostling, trying to get one last glimpse of England's shores while narrowing their eyes against the glare of an early morning sun glowing orange behind skeins of wispy cloud. Some held their phones at the end of an outstretched arm, posing for selfies as they leaned against the railings nonchalantly, heads thrown back like Jack or Rose in the film *Titanic*.

The name Rose made me think of my twin, and my heart beat faster and gave me an odd guilty pang as I wondered if she'd woken yet and seen that I was gone. I took a cursory glance at my phone, but there were no text messages demanding to know where I was and no missed calls. I fully intended to text later once I was properly on my way. Once the sight of English land had gone, and there was no turning back. Well, not for a while anyway.

Thinking about it, though, nobody would suspect I'd gone until later this afternoon. Rose tended to sleep late on a Saturday, whereas I was up with the lark and out walking at least until lunch time, St. Thomas a Becket Church at Warblington, the cemetery, and the seashore being some of my favorite places to explore. I hadn't heard Rose come in the night before but had seen her this morning slumbering like Sleeping Beauty, her duvet discarded on the floor like a snow drift, and puffing breath soft and hissy between clenched teeth. I cursed each creaking stair as I padded downstairs and across the old worn tiles in the hallway to slip quietly out of the back door and to the shed where I'd hidden my rucksack.

The early morning bus from Emsworth had meandered along, swaying from side to side like a drunk, the muddy stench from Langstone sneaking through the windows like marmite—you know, you either love it or you hate it. Me? It brought back childhood memories, so I loved it. The roads, fairly quiet at this time of day, started to get a little busier as we came into Cosham, and from there, only straggly queuing as we finally arrived in Portsmouth. Climbing aboard the ferry, shuffling along amongst the crowds, I thought about the B&B that I'd booked in St. Malo, picked totally at random just because I liked the name. La Petite Amelia. The words rolled off my tongue, sweet as honey, La Petite Amelia. I couldn't wait to see it.

Once Portsmouth had finally disappeared from the horizon, and there was only an endless sea beneath an endless sky, I made my way inside and, stomach gurgling like faulty plumbing, ordered hot chocolate and a flaky croissant at a small bustling café. Sitting down near a window, I peered out at the rolling and swelling of the glassy green waves as the boat peaked and rolled. I'd thought that I'd be nauseated, but I felt okay, just a bit lonely without the comforting presence of Rose at my side. I wasn't used to a great empty space that at the moment felt impossible to fill.

Drinking the last of my hot chocolate, I wandered back out onto the deck, the swaying of the ferry making me lurch like a drunk and, resting my rucksack at my feet, leaned against the rail and gazed out to sea, idly watching the feathery white-tipped waves slapping against the sides of the ferry and seagulls diving for fish that glinted silver beneath the water. The deck was almost deserted now as everybody had gone inside for breakfast, and the odor of frying bacon and eggs, mixed with the heady smell of filtered coffee, filled the air.

I sensed rather than saw a presence at my side, a tall

figure wearing a long dark coat open to reveal jeans and a white T-shirt bearing the words Thin Lizzy in big square letters. He wore a thin striped scarf wound casually around his neck like one of our upper-grade students. He was vaping, clutching the machine as though his life depended on it, taking sharp intakes of breath, exhaling a flowery sweetish smell that snaked through the air like one of Mum's scented candles.

We turned in unison and smiled. I noticed his eyes were as green and glassy as the sea that swelled and heaved around us.

"Hi," he said, formally holding out a hand. "Blake... Blake Edwards."

His hand felt warm and dry as I gripped it and said, "Ruby Deacon," for some reason giving a little bow of my head. He grinned before picking up a guitar by its long slender neck, which, unnoticed by me, had been propped up beside him, and bursting into song.

"'Goodbye Ruby Tuesday, who could hang a name on you, when you change with every new day, still gonna miss you....' Don't mind me," he said, "I like to sing." He placed the guitar carefully, almost reverently, back against the railings, keeping it close to his body.

"Wow," I said, delighted. "Nobody's ever sung my song before...thank you."

"Are you called Ruby Tuesday?" he asked, taking a step back, his hands held up in front of him. "Please say you are. I've never met a Ruby Tuesday before."

I nodded. "Yes, Ruby Tuesday Deacon."

"Wow. Are your parents hippies? Big fans of the

Stones?" He turned fully towards me, resting his body comfortably on the railings and lacing his hands in front of him as if he were in for the long haul.

I mulled over this for a few seconds before saying, "Hmm, hippies? Not any more. But fans of the Rolling Stones? Yes, definitely, especially my dad."

"Yeah, they're great, and these guys." He pointed to the band name on his T-shirt. "A pity bands today aren't like them. They played proper music." He thought for a minute or two, chewing his lower lip, which incidentally was as glossy and red as a ripe strawberry, before saying, his hand held to his heart, "RIP…real music is dead!"

We both nodded, silently agreeing with each other. I even put my hand to my heart as well, for God's sake!

"I know we're only young," he carried on. "You can't be more than twenty?"

"I'm twenty-two," I told him.

He nodded. "And I'm thirty—just. But really, today's music has no soul. I envy older people for being there at the right time and in the right place, for their enjoyment of their music." He spoke so passionately and gave me a smile so charming I felt as if something pierced my heart, and then abruptly, he changed the subject. "Are you on holiday?" he asked. "Travelling?" He nodded his head towards my rucksack, slumped like a down and out at my feet.

"Yeah, just taking a week or two to explore France," I said casually, putting on an act for his benefit of being grown up, a seasoned traveller, not how I really felt—gauche and unsure, nervous, and afraid of my own shadow. "You?" I asked.

"Just pottering about," he replied. "Seeing where the wind blows me."

He laughed, faint wrinkles appearing at the corners of his eyes and showing even white teeth between the blackness of the beard that coated his upper lip and chin. His hair was black too, even sort of bluey in the sunlight, parted in the middle, springing in wings from his forehead and reaching his shoulders.

He reminded me a tiny bit of James, but he was older and more self-assured, maybe a little battered as if, so far, his life had been a long hard road. He took a deep drag on the vape machine and, watching me closely, said, "Trying to crack a forty a day cigarette habit, and man is it hard." He shook his head wearily.

Before I could reply, my phone beeped, alerting me to a text message. *Oh no*, I thought. *This is it. It'll be from Rose.* "Excuse me," I said and turned away slightly, shielding the screen from the sun with a cupped hand.

Hey Ruby, if you're still out walking, go to Smith & Vosper for bread, will you? Mum's orders. Thanx, xxx.

I smiled to myself and replaced my phone in my pocket, thinking, *Oh well, they obviously don't know I've gone as yet.*

"A problem?" he asked.

"No, not really, just my sister asking me to take bread home."

"Hmm, don't you think your sister's bread will be moldy by the time you get back?" I shrugged, and he frowned and said, in a silly mock French accent, "Hmm. I think you've got a story to tell." He glanced at his watch. "Hey, look, it's almost lunchtime. Let's go get a beer, and you can tell me all."

The bar was crowded and noisy, and the music blaring through massive speakers was "New Music," as Blake said with a grin, batting at the air with his hands as if it was of no account. So we went out onto the deck and made ourselves comfortable in plastic chairs in a quiet corner, cradling bottles of ice-cold beer in our hands. The sun was very warm now, and the deck crowded with people either milling about or laying on loungers or towels soaking up the rays. Children ran and played, shrieking and laughing.

Blake took off his coat and scarf and laid them carefully at our feet, along with his guitar. I noticed that his arms were tanned and covered in tiny light hairs like down. He leaned closer towards me, his forearms on his thighs and, occasionally swigging from the bottle, invited me to talk. His attention solely on me was intoxicating and, together with the lulling movement of the boat and the ice-cold beer, before I knew what I was doing, I was telling him everything. Everything about Rose and the job in the library, James and my need for freedom, my need to not be a twin for a while but to just be myself.

"Well then, Ruby Tuesday," he said when I came to a stuttering finale, "You are doing absolutely the right thing." He clinked his bottle against mine in a toast and, picking up his guitar, began playing the opening bars of "Ruby Tuesday." We sang and played, an interested crowd gathering around us, until the afternoon passed us by, and everybody dispersed to the sides of the ferry to look at the beauty of St. Malo, gilded gold in the evening sunshine as we glided into port. My phone had buzzed several times, so I knew I had an important phone call to make as soon as I arrived at the B&B. Shrugging my rucksack onto my back, I followed Blake's retreating figure as we made our way off the boat and onto French land. And wow, how beautiful it was with its tiny inlets of sandy beaches and tall, dignified houses.

Despite the almost constant buzzing of my phone, I felt a strange exhilaration and took several deep breaths of the fresh salty air as I gazed around. I noticed that Blake was a little apart from me now, his phone clamped to his ear. He paced up and down, talking animatedly, his guitar firmly in his hand and his scarf and coat hooked over his arm. I felt unsure of what to do next. Should I go off alone and look for my B&B, or should I wait for him? I glanced at my phone again—another couple of texts from Rose. I really needed to be somewhere private where I could call and speak to her and Mum as well.

My heart lightened as I saw Blake striding towards me. He did a courteous little bow of the head and, taking hold of my hand, kissed the palm quite erotically, I thought, sending pleasant little shivers hurtling through my body before saying in his silly mock French accent, "Thank you, Ruby. You have made what could have been a boring voyage into something special. I hope we meet again."

"Oh yes, me too," I said, giggling girlishly, standing there like a dumb fool waiting for the verbal exchange of phone numbers or, as with James, a scrap of paper to be pressed into my outstretched hand.

He kissed the tips of his fingers, and with a flourish, proffered me an airborne salute. "*Au revoir, mon cheri....*" And without further ado, he turned his back and walked away, swallowed up quickly by the hungry crowds.

Chapter Four

I awoke the following morning, wrapped like a mummy in the thin duvet, unsure at first of where I was and expecting at any moment to hear Rose's ragged breathing from the other side of the room divider. But of course, there was no room divider, and I was alone at the B&B La Petite Amelia in St. Malo. Slipping out of bed, I went to the window, carefully rolled up the cream blind, and peered out at the garden. It was a proper garden, a smooth lawn and well-stocked fragrant borders, the B&B being a big old house set within its own large grounds. It also happened to be on a hiking trail, as well as being within walking distance of the beaches and the town. I couldn't have picked a better place to stay. As a matter of fact, it reminded me of home. And as well as that, the proprietors, Amelia and Georges, had made me feel so welcome when I'd arrived late last night straight from the ferry port.

Stretching and yawning, the events of the day before

suddenly crashed into my mind, and once again, I saw the tall figure of Blake Edwards walking away from me, probably never to be seen again. How weird was that? I'd told him everything, things I would never have said if it hadn't been for the two beers loosening my tongue and making me natter on and on like an old washer woman. It wasn't just that, though—he was a good listener. He seemed interested, and he'd told me I was doing the right thing, that I wouldn't regret taking the time out to be alone and think about my life and where I was going.

He'd been attractive too, I thought wryly, more so than James in some ways, although in an older, more beat up sort of way. He looked as though he'd been through hard times and that perhaps he even had problems. Why that should be more interesting to me than a younger man of twenty-three fresh out of college, with a good job and no worries, was absolutely beyond me. Maybe it was his singing…or his serenading me with the song "Ruby Tuesday," and his silly mock French accent…or perhaps it was his sexy sea-green eyes and stubbly beard. Who knows?

Anyway, I didn't come all the way to France on my own to become infatuated with a man—in fact, that was the one thing I should be avoiding at all costs. My head had been turned. Oh my God, how weak I was to fall for the first eligible male that came along. I would be keeping myself to myself from now on, and there would definitely be no more confiding in handsome strangers, that was for sure. Today I would lace up my walking boots and take to the hills and dales—were there hills and dales in France?—and not, I repeat not, sit around drinking beer and singing silly songs.

No, not even silly love songs.

Once the chastising of myself, the sheer flagellation of myself, was over — I almost expected to see blood oozing from my already tanned skin — my mind wandered to the conversation I'd had with Rose. The conversation I had dreaded but knew I had to have once I eventually found my B&B. The shouting and the tears, all because I wouldn't be there for a couple of weeks to accompany her to Hayling Island, or Southsea, or Prinstead, or to try surfing at the Witterings. I was selfish and mean not to have told her. How dare I sneak off like that! Was I crazy!

"You got the job," I felt like saying to her, "And I got the holiday." But of course, I didn't say that. It was my own fault — I'd left the job wide open. I kept quiet most of the time, just pointing out when I could get a word in edgeways that it was only for a couple of weeks and that after that, I would be back, and there'd still be plenty of time to do all those things together before school started again.

The conversation with Mum was totally different. She said that both she and Dad were proud of me for being so adventurous and that there was no question I was doing the right thing. Also, they understood why I had sneaked away as I had, especially now, having seen firsthand Rose's reaction to it. Everybody should go find themselves at some point in their lives, she told me. She spouted out a few very badly pronounced French words, which made me laugh, and told me to be careful and to ring every couple of days…and to text too. She spoke loudly and clearly over the background noise of Rose's sobbing. "I have a full orchestra behind me," she said, "And it's playing far too many encores." Now that did crack me up.

~*~

The next few days passed in a haze of walking, sightseeing, swimming in impossibly warm clear water, and sunning myself on many of St. Malo's pretty little beaches. I loved walking through the town and looking at the historic walls and cobblestoned streets, as well as wandering the old town with its long string of cafes and restaurants and then relaxing on St. Malo's most famous sandy beach, the Plage Du Sillon. It was a problem though that, however hard I tried not to, I kept a vigilant eye out for the tall figure of Blake Edwards, but he was nowhere to be seen. Sometimes I had the strange feeling I'd imagined our encounter on the ferry, and that he didn't exist at all, or if he ever had, he'd disappeared into thin air just like the invisible man.

Convinced that I'd succeeded and banished him from my mind for good, and in any case would probably never see him again, one evening almost a week after my arrival, I decided to walk into the old town and wander the little shops for gifts for Rose and Mum and Dad to take back with me. I decided I might also have a bite to eat and a drink at one of the many bars that lined the streets, as I'd eaten at the B&B every night and fancied a change.

I waved goodbye to a few of the guests sitting in the garden basking in the evening sunshine and enjoying coffee and cakes while Amelia and Georges toiled in the kitchens cooking the evening meal. The walk into town was pleasant, and I felt good wearing a pretty sundress, trainers on my feet for ease of walking, and a small rucksack on my back carrying water, phone, and purse. Oh, and I always carried a French phrase book just in case. I'd caught the sun and felt tanned and fit as I strolled along.

The town was busy, and I immersed myself in the crowds going from one shop to another, looking at all the beautiful things on display. Such unusual jewelry, scarves, and hats. So many things to choose from for a woman, but for a man? What on earth could I get Dad? Ah, chocolate! Such beautiful shops selling unusual types of chocolate. My eyes on stalks, I gazed in the shop windows, unsure, as yet, of what to buy, although I was pretty sure of scarves for Mum and Rose and chocolate or whiskey for Dad.

First things first, I thought as I caught sight of a micro bar called simply La Bar. Ducking inside, I sat at a table and ordered a glass of red wine, taking a cursory glance at the menu as I waited. It was a tiny place very similar to the micro bars that had sprouted up recently in England and was very cozy and welcoming, with soft lighting and gentle background music.

"Madam," said the young bartender as he placed the glass of wine on a mat in front of me. "You eat?"

"Yes, please," I said and, referring to the menu, ordered a cheese quiche with a green salad, something simple I could order without having too much trouble speaking the language. I had my school girl French, but not much else.

"No problem, madam," he said politely as I thanked him for the wine and took a sip. While waiting, I texted Rose, telling her I was in a bar alone drinking wine and was just about to enjoy some food. I told her I was okay but missed her and Mum and Dad and would be back within a week. She'd been very mean with her texts since we'd spoken last week, so it was hit and miss as to whether she would get back to me. I sent a similar text to Mum and dropped my phone back into my bag just as the young bartender brought my food, which looked really good.

"Merci," I said, but instead of leaving straight away so I could eat, the young bartender hovered around the table, obviously trying to tell me something.

"Madam, please you...umm...."

Puzzled, I asked him, "Yes?" putting out my hands palms up.

"We have...um...singer tonight?"

I nodded vigorously and repeated his words. "You have a singer tonight?"

"Oui, here." He indicated the area I was sitting in.

"Ah. You want me to move for the singer to sit here?" I began to stand up.

A look of relief passed over his face. "Oui, madam." He indicated some other seats. "Madam, here." He escorted me to the seat, fussily fluttering around as I moved from one place to the other and settled down to eat. "Look." He pointed at a poster I hadn't noticed tacked to the wall beside me. "Look, madam. Singer here...Mr. Blake. Guitar...." He held out his left arm and began to strum against his chest with his right hand while putting a sort of rock star look on his face. "Guitar, madam."

Looking closely at the poster, I saw a familiar face. A face that, yes, I had to admit, I was very pleased to see. I'd really wanted another look at the combination of sea-green eyes, shoulder-length dark hair, and stubbly beard.

"Mr. Blake?" I asked the bartender, pointing at the

person on the poster. A man posed almost seductively on a settee piled with cushions, cradling a guitar in his arms like a baby, the rock star pout that the bartender had tried to copy on his face. He would definitely make a good model.

"Oui, madam, Mr. Blake." He began to walk back to the bar. "Bon appetite, madam."

"Merci! What time Mr. Blake here?" I asked, tapping at my watch.

"Now," said the bartender, shrugging his shoulders. "Maybe. When he comes…."

I grinned at how laid back they were and turned to my food. As I ate, the place began to fill up, and a knot of people crowded around the bar to order drinks, some of them looking intently at the menu. I noticed that a young girl and an older woman had joined the bartender and were frantically running around trying to disperse the heaving queue.

A man appeared at the table I'd vacated, moved it aside, and began to set up a couple of small speakers and a microphone on a stand. He did a cursory squealing sound check that reverberated around the room, setting my teeth on edge, nodded with approval, and wandered off into the shadows.

After eating every last morsel of food, I checked my phone. I had a text from Mum telling me to be careful in a bar alone but to have a good time—nothing from Rose as yet. Wow, she was definitely playing hard to get. I had the distinct feeling that it would take a lot for her to forgive me for this little escapade, as she called it. Well, it was too bad. I was enjoying myself, and to prove it, I drained the last drops of wine and asked the passing bartender if he could possibly bring me another, which he did with a little bow and a "You are welcome, madam."

More people started to pack into the bar, and an older couple, after many hand gestures and head nodding, sat at my table, thanking me profusely by raising their glasses and their thumbs in that age-old "I'm okay" gesture. It was very warm now, and the crowd restless and excited. Perspiration gathered at my hairline and trickled down my cheeks like tears. Snippets of conversation popped out at me.

"Yes, Mr. Blake."

"Very good."

"Where is he?"

"Do you think he will come?"

Just when I'd given up all hope, a large dark shape appeared in the doorway, and the bar fell silent. He ran lightly down the entrance steps, the neck of his guitar firmly clasped in his clenched hand. He wore jeans and a red T-shirt, this time the words T-Rex picked out in black lettering on the front. The brightness of the red looked good against his tanned skin and black hair and beard. At this moment, he reminded me of those great front men Michael Hutchence, Freddie Mercury, or Jim Morrison. He went immediately to the microphone, and without further ado, played straight into the opening bars of "Ruby Tuesday." The crowd went wild.

Chapter Five

For two days, it had rained…thank God for my trusty rain slicker. Sheets and sheets of silver rain that drummed against the windows of the La Petite Amelia and soaked into the beautiful gardens, into the emerald green lawn and the rich flowery borders. Not the icy cold rain that soaked into your bones, the spoiler of holidays, but warm, gentle rain that allowed you to walk the sands or paddle in the glassy shallows, where tiny silver fish darted amongst your toes, or sit beneath an umbrella eating fresh salty cockles and sipping red wine.

After the two rainy days, the deluge stopped, and the sun appeared shining bright yellow, the sky blue and cloudless. Seagulls flew lazily over gently rolling waves and, taking a towel and all the other necessary things for an afternoon at the beach, I made my way down to the warm sands, where wearily I laid down and closed my eyes. The beach was almost deserted today, only the lapping of the waves and the faint cawing of the gulls breaking the silence. Really, I was supposed to have moved on from La Petite Amelia after a week or two but, because I was so happy there and in such close proximity to the lovely beaches, shops, and bars, I kept extending my stay. I didn't know what it would take to make me leave this place, but it would have to be something big! And okay, my job in a few weeks' time, of course.

The beeping of my phone brought me out of my almost comatose state and peering intently at the screen, I saw that it was a message from Blake. Yes, you read that perfectly well, a message from Blake. We had exchanged phone numbers more than a week ago on the night he caused hysterical mayhem with his guitar playing in the little micro pub La Bar — another reason to stay at La Petite Amelia?

Hey Ruby Tuesday, where are you?

I texted back straight away. *Recovering from last night on the tiny beach near my B&B. Where are you?*

Another beep. *Don't move. I'm on my way.*

I felt a sudden panic and sat up abruptly, gazing down at my slim tanned body clad in a new pink bikini, the low rise bottoms and bra top edged with silver sparkles, bought only the day before in a very exclusive boutique in St. Malo. Blake had been there too and had assured me that it was a bikini not only fit for a queen but a great fit for Ruby Tuesday. Taking a quick look in a tiny hand mirror that I'd stuffed into my bag, I decided I looked okay, even though the sun had brought out freckles that coated my nose like sugar frosting on a cake. I'd tied my thick hair up on top of my head with a large pink comb, giving it the appearance of the crown of a pineapple. "Oh well, whatever…."

"Wow, you look great! What did I tell you about that bikini? I knew you'd look great in it. You've got a fabulous figure."

Raising a hand and shielding my eyes against the sun, I saw that Blake had suddenly materialized in front of me. He looked cool as usual, wearing denim shorts and yet another band T-shirt, a green one. Queen was printed across the front in white letters, together with the band logo and an image of Freddie Mercury when he sported his long flowing locks.

I smiled. "Thank you. Yeah, I'm glad I bought it now. God, Blake, how many band T-shirts do you have?"

"Enough for every great band that ever existed," he told me as he unrolled his towel and plonked himself down, giving me a sidelong glance. "And that's a lot."

He began to recite them all slowly and carefully, to which I said, "Yeah, okay, okay…."

Grinning, he leaned over and lingeringly kissing my shoulder, saying, "Mm, you taste salty, Ruby Tuesday."

I batted him away, saying, "Oh Blake," but he held on tight and said into my neck, so muffled I could barely hear, "Have you enjoyed the past week?"

"Of course I have. Why?" I was very conscious of the shushing of the waves onto the shore and the crying of the gulls as I waited for his reply.

He pulled back slightly and gazed at me, into my eyes, the green of his boring into the blue of mine. Cupping my face between his hands, he said, "What will happen when you go back home? Will you take up with James?"

I frowned and pulled back a little, saying, "I've no idea what will happen when I go back home. Nothing has gone on between me and James, probably nothing ever will. I'm just enjoying myself here with you."

"A holiday romance?" he asked.

I laughed and, trying to be oh so worldly-wise and in control, said flippantly, "Yes, a holiday romance."

He laughed too and pulled me tightly into his arms again and placed his lips on mine, not for the first time by any means. We'd shared our first kiss after his first performance at La Bar and had been inseparable ever since. He'd been pleased to see me, he said, and had hoped we'd meet again, although never explaining why he had walked away and left me in the first place. I was sceptical at first, believing he would have done absolutely nothing to find me, suspecting even that he already had a girlfriend. He was a good looking eligible man—in fact, too good-looking, suave, and sophisticated to bother with me. And who had he been speaking to on his mobile when we left the ferry? It had to be a woman, surely.

I hadn't asked him outright, but after all, he knew everything about me, about James, and about the couple of school girl romances I'd had which had come to nothing, so surely he would tell me if there was a woman in his life. Wouldn't he? The only thing he'd told me was that he'd had a girlfriend a few years ago called Janice, but they'd split when she moved away with her parents to Greece. He'd had the opportunity to go with the family but had decided to stay where he was, in London, because musically that's where it was at—as he said.

He told me that he had set up a band called The London Boys, but when they had no luck in getting a recording contract to keep body and soul together, he managed to get a job writing advertising copy in a fairly well-established firm in the city while still trying to make it in music. He also said he'd been writing his own songs so he wouldn't have to play covers. "Although," he said with a grin, "Some of the covers I played went down very well!" Now that he had gained such popularity in La Bar, I thought it had reignited his interest in fame and fortune, and he'd been thinking of searching for like-minded people so he could form another band. Oh God, if only I could sing, or at least play an instrument! I could be Ruby Tuesday, a modern-day Debbie Harry.

I decided to push all my worries about Blake having another girlfriend into the back of my mind and just get on with enjoying every minute I spent with him. After all, he was with me right here and right now. I know I said earlier that I shouldn't be getting involved with anybody, that I was going to keep away from all men, but I just couldn't help myself. He was good company, funny, and entertaining, with lots of stories to tell. He serenaded me with his singing and guitar playing, and above all, kissed me as though he really meant it, with real passion and feeling. But sometimes, unfortunately, he acted quite remote and stand-offish, as if he were somewhere else entirely. A strange combination. What was happening to me? Was I falling in love? And was Blake too? I couldn't tell.

The time sped away, and before I realized it, two weeks had flown by, and then another week, and then another. By this time, I was being hounded with text messages from Rose, tearfully demanding to know why I hadn't returned, saying that the holidays were almost over and we hadn't had time together. Maliciously, she told me that James had been seen around in Emsworth with a girl who was on holiday with Vanessa, that they spent all their time together and, yes, that girl could have been me.

All this left me cold. I didn't care that James had been seen with another girl. I remember only a few short weeks ago being worried that I might want to text him while I was away, but even though I'd put his number into my phone, I'd never had the urge to do that. And as much as I cared for Rose, I didn't want to go for days out with her all the time. I wanted to be with Blake. At the moment, we were spending all our time together, so much so that it was increasingly difficult to part at the end of an evening, and I'd lost count of the times I'd contemplated sneaking him into my room at La Petite Amelia. Only my great regard for Amelia and Georges prevented me from doing that. Thinking about it all now, if it hadn't been for the tearful phone call from Rose as I neared my fourth week away, I wonder if I would ever have plucked up the courage to go home at all.~*~

I was miserable this time as I sat in the same small busy café on the ferry, sipping at a barely warm hot chocolate and once again watching the glassy green waves heaving outside the little window. On the way over to France, I'd been excited and buoyed up, looking forward to my impending adventure. Now I was just down, depressed even, and worried about what would happen next. I couldn't eat this time — I could just about handle the hot chocolate. I had no appetite, not since leaving Blake and not after fully taking stock of the news that Rose had told me on the phone. Unbelievable news, news that I couldn't make heads or tails of — news I'd told Blake about in a shocked voice brimmed with tears that spurted from my swollen eyes and dripped down my flushed cheeks. I hated being like this in front of Blake, but I couldn't help myself. Along with the hated rain slicker, it was definitely not my best look.

He'd comforted me as well as he could, telling me that things would make more sense when I got back and could speak properly to Mum because the news had more bearing on Mum—not Dad or Rose, but Mum. Rose's voice had come clear as a bell through my mobile. I'd pressed it hard to my waiting ear, preparing myself for more ranting about why I still wasn't home. We were in La Bar surrounded by the usual expectant audience waiting for Blake to do his nightly performance, sitting close together, holding hands, his thumb idly massaging the palm of my hand. It was amazing, but we couldn't keep our hands from each other.

"Ruby, you've got to come home. Our brother turned up at the house yesterday right out of the blue—it's pandemonium here. Mum's crying and Dad's distraught. If you can spare the time for us, please come, Ruby."

"Our brother? But Rose, we haven't got a brother." I said this while thinking, '*If you can spare the time for us*'? *What did she mean by that*?

"Oh yes, we have, Ruby. Big family secret. Will you come home?"

"Yes," I said immediately. "Of course I will."

Rose had already told me that Dad would pick me up from the ferry port, and I expected her to be there too, but there was just Dad waiting for me, his face expectant, searching the crowds and then lighting up as he saw me and took me into his arms. Despite the fact that I was with Dad and would soon see Mum and Rose, I felt suddenly down and forlorn, and the fact that my holiday really had ended began to sink in. I just hoped deep in my heart that the relationship I had with Blake wasn't at an end too. And to make matters even worse, the sun had slipped away behind black-edged clouds, and a drizzly rain began to fall.

"Oh, Ruby, it's good to see you. Sorry you've had to cut your holiday short."

I studied him closely. He looked just the same — fit, tanned, handsome even. From what I'd heard, he had most of his female patients in a tizzy. Yeah, same old Dad.

"No, Dad, don't say that. I should have been back ages ago."

"Why?" he asked, gently pushing me away from him, arms outstretched, his hands on my shoulders. "You're of age. As long as you're back to take up your job in two weeks' time, then that's fine."

I smiled. "Thanks, Dad. I'm sorry I sneaked off the way I did, but —"

"It's okay, Ruby," he replied, grinning a little. "I would think that sometimes being a twin is hard going?"

"Yes. It's great, but yes, sometimes it's stifling."

Throwing my rucksack into the trunk, we got in the car. The doors shut with a thunk, and after a minute or two of silence, just the sound of the rain pattering against the roof, Dad said, "I'm sure you know what this is all about. I know Rose has told you something. Your brother — well, your stepbrother, um, Michael — turned up out of the blue. He's been searching for your mum for a couple of years, apparently."

"Wow," I said. "Will I be able to meet him?"

"Yeah, of course, you can. He's staying at the Coal Exchange at the moment. He's got a really nice room there — obviously because there's no space in the house, no spare room."

"Rose said you were distraught, Dad. I don't understand. When did Mum have him? Is he yours too?"

"I was upset at first, Ruby, until I talked properly to your mum. Before I knew the circumstances. No, he's not mine. I.... Well, Ruby, I knew nothing about him — your mum chose not to tell me. Before we knew each other properly, your mum went missing for a while, during the six weeks school holidays — unknown to me. And don't forget I was very young too, only sixteen. Your mum was pregnant and had gone to have the baby. When he was born, they took him away from her — she only had a glimpse. She was heartbroken. She did tell me, though, that she made the decision to have the baby adopted. She said that Nan and Grandad thought it would be for the best."

"Did Mum have a change of heart when she saw him?"

Dad nodded, a tight smile on his face, his eyes a piercing steely blue. "But it was too late then. Arrangements had been made. He was adopted by a couple from Swansea in Wales, and that's where he's lived the whole time." He looked at me and smiled. "He has a bit of an accent. Anyway, a couple of years ago, his adopted mum died. His adopted dad had died a few years before that, so he felt free to go ahead and search for his birth mum. And the rest is history."

"Does he know who his dad is?" I asked carefully.

"I know nothing about that," replied Dad. "Mum will

know, obviously, but I don't know whether she'll tell you. I haven't asked her. But it was a long time ago…." He let the rest of the sentence hang in the air, so I knew I would have to take this up with Mum if I wanted any answers there. I felt a sudden tremor from my pocket and realized my phone had beeped with a text message. Giving Dad an apologetic glance, I took a brief look and, with a lifting of my spirits, saw that it was from Blake, asking if I was okay.

"Holiday romance?" asked Dad, giving me the eye.

"You don't miss a trick, do you, Dad?" I teased.

"Come on," he said as he turned on the engine, bringing the car to life. I watched the windscreen wipers cut a smooth arc across the rain-smeared window. "Let's go home and see Mum."

I nodded and put my mobile back into my bag. I would text Blake later.

Dad shook his head slowly. "And as much as Rose is getting pretty smitten with her new brother, she's crazy to see you, Ruby."

I smiled and said, "Yeah, it'll be good to see her too."

Chapter Six

September and the start of a new school term. I was at work on the reception desk, which was crazy busy with parents of new students ringing to make sure their little darlings were doing okay. I'd been looking out for the new ones, all those little fish swimming against the tide in such a big pond. It was a big, daunting step up from a primary to a senior school, so I could understand the parent's worries. No doubt I would be the same one day — if I was ever lucky enough to have kids, that is.

Giving a big sigh, I thought how work had always kept me busy and focused, but today it just didn't seem to be working. Also, it didn't help that outside, the sun was shining, and thoughts of St. Malo kept flitting through my mind. However hard I tried, I just couldn't make them go away. I could smell the salty tang of the sea and heard the cawing of the gulls — because, of course, French seagulls were completely different from the ones in Emsworth, right? I couldn't help thinking about the view of the beautiful garden from my room at La Petite Amelia, and the little sandy inlets where I used to swim, and far out at sea, little fishing boats bobbing on the waves. But most of all, of course, I thought of Blake.

Yes, I thought of Blake. I thought of his lovely green eyes as they looked into mine, imagined the touch of his fingers stroking my skin, the taste of his lips on mine. And I heard his voice, either speaking with his silly French accent or singing, serenading me with his guitar. We'd been in touch, texted a lot and spoken a couple of times, and he'd made heartfelt promises that we would see each other again soon. That when he could, he would leave St. Malo and come to Emsworth to see me. I was hopeful on that score, but I'd had worries since I came back home, mainly with Rose. And of course, there was Michael to get used to. And Mum. Something was different. Something had changed. Very subtly, but it was there all the same. Waiting in the wings, like a drama to be played out.

Rose had started her new job in the library, and I glimpsed her flitting backwards and forwards, smart in the uniform of black trousers and a short-sleeved blue and white blouse, carrying piles of books or official looking forms, sometimes accompanying students from the library to classrooms and vice versa. I heard her voice, sometimes raised sternly, sometimes with a girlish giggle, but always — what's the expression? — kind but firm. She looked relaxed yet purposeful as if she was enjoying herself. In between phone calls, I tried to catch her eye, to smile and nod, to let her know that everything was okay, that I supported her in the job and was happy, but she wouldn't look at me. The averted gaze seemed to say, "Ruby, I'm far too busy in my important new job to bother with you." She was ignoring me. I had to come to terms with it. My twin, my other half, the other side of my face, my Rose, was ignoring me.

She'd been cool since I'd got back, and Dad's comment about Rose being crazy to see me had definitely been wrong. I don't know whether or not it was a coincidence that we were never in our room, awake, together. She went out in the evenings with the usual gang but never asked me, and I was usually asleep when she came in, and then she was asleep when I went out early in the mornings. She barely asked any questions about my holiday, my adventure, and because of that, I'd not uttered a word — in fact, I'd told no one, as yet — about Blake.

Dad had made the remark about a holiday romance when he picked me up, but I hadn't followed up on it, and he hadn't asked again. It was as if everybody was too wrapped up with our stepbrother now. And anyway, I didn't want to look a fool if it all came to nothing, and I never heard from Blake again. Oh my God, what a downer I was on. Holidays were supposed to do you good, perk you up. In this case, though, it seemed that the reverse was true and that I was slowly sinking deeper and deeper into a pit of despair.

Lunch time came, and I made a tentative foray into the cafeteria. I didn't usually go in there, as I brought my own lunch and, if it was a sunny day, always sat outside at the wooden benches set aside for staff, private from the students. Rose was in there so deep in conversation with Katie, the library manager, that I didn't like to intrude. They were tucking into bowls of tuna salad and sipping steaming coffee from plastic cups.

I made a half-hearted unsuccessful attempt to catch her eye before wandering outside, where I sat at a bench with Jo and a couple of the girls from the Student Reception Team, who were more than willing to engage in conversation about our respective holidays. They were also eager to find out why Rose was "swanning it around" in the library while I was still "stuck at the reception desk" — their words, not mine. I told them I'd changed my mind about the job and felt that Rose would be far better at it than me.

"Don't you be so sure, Ruby," pointed out Lynne. "It's only her first week on the job, and she's throwing her weight around already. That job was yours."

An opened bag of crisps lay on the table, from which they all picked at regular intervals.

"Throwing her weight around?" I bit into a sandwich and chewed thoughtfully. "I find that hard to believe. Rose isn't like that."

The three of them exchanged glances before Lynne said, "We hadn't really intended to say anything to you, Ruby, but…well, yes, she is like that. She's already been into Student Reception this morning, demanding to know why some literature quiz sheets weren't ready and waiting on her desk this morning. First week back too. Did she think we were in here over the holidays, laminating the sheets for her?"

Quick to defend my twin, I said, "Once she's settled down, she'll be fine. She'll be trying to prove herself to Katie."

"Yeah, well, Katie won't be happy if she behaves that way towards us. But okay, we'll see how it goes," mused Paula. She took a sip of milkshake, banana by the smell of it, and went on. "But she's going to have to come down from that pedestal she's put herself on, or she won't be very popular."

"Yeah," stated Lynne. "She needs to understand that kindness and respect towards others is the way to go around here. She's so different from you, Ruby."

"Actually," said Paula, giving me a sidelong glance, "Maybe you could have a word with her? Put her on the right track before she makes a total mess of it."

Almost choking on my coffee, I spluttered, "I'll see what I can do. But…well, I don't like to interfere, especially where Rose is concerned." I almost mentioned home and our new found stepbrother and all the complications that seemed to have arisen because of him. But I decided against it and clamped my mouth shut, bam, like one of those cockle shells that Blake and I used to find lying around on the beach, razor-sharp enough to cut your toes if you weren't careful.

"Yeah," said Lynne. "Do you know what, Ruby? If you two didn't look so alike, I'd question whether you're even sisters, let alone twins."

I decided to ignore that remark and carefully folded the foil my sandwiches had been wrapped in and placed it in my bag before saying, "Anyway, what happened to all the other people that were going to apply for the library job? The internal applicants?"

Both Lynne and Paula shrugged, and Jo replied, "Not sure. I think only one other person applied. Angie, I think. You know, the girl from Attendance? But apparently, she didn't have enough experience with books."

We gazed around at each other and laughed. "Experience with books? What does that mean?"

I went back to my desk at reception feeling slightly more lighthearted, cheered up in a way by the conversation with the girls, even though it had shown a somewhat darker side to Rose. I was also on a bit of a high with the arrival of a text message from Blake, telling me he had another regular booking at a club called Platform 99, which, he said, was a really cool place. And from his advertisement for band members, he'd had responses from a drummer and a bass player, and he would be meeting them this very evening in La Bar.

Wow, was he really on his way to fame and fortune? While I was pleased for him, another darker side of me had vague misgivings about the good-looking rock star, Blake Edwards, being besieged by fans, eager women of all curvy shapes and sizes, mostly far more pretty and attractive than me. Would he be tempted by the adoration of his fans, or even, far worse still, tempted into liaisons with groupies? A hot wave of panic swept over me, and I took a deep breath to steady myself. I must put thoughts like that out of my mind — otherwise, it would drive me mad.

The rest of the day passed in a busy blur and, as soon as the bell sounded for the end of the day, I grabbed my bag and jacket and made a beeline for the door. I saw Rose briefly in the milling crowd of students and teachers making her way alongside Katie to the parking lot. Perhaps Katie was giving her a lift home. Rose knew I always walked, so she definitely wouldn't be searching me out to accompany her. I texted Blake before I set off, a short chatty text telling him I was pleased he had another booking and potential new band mates but that I missed him and wished I were there. I even made a joke about joining the band and playing the maracas, just as Jim Morrison used to while lead singer with the Doors.

Thoughts of Rose and the comments made by the Student Reception girls ran through my mind as I began the walk home. The weather was sunny and warm but, in readiness for the autumn, leaves of bright ambers, golds, and reds pried themselves from the bony twisted branches of the trees and twirled gently to the ground. I knew Rose could be bossy at times, particularly with me, but I didn't think I'd ever known her to be that way with other people. Thinking about it, though, this was her first really responsible job. Okay, she'd worked in fast food outlets and bakery shops, but this was a school, and maybe different rules and attitudes applied, particularly as she was working with children. Perhaps I really should speak to her about it before she did, as the girls said, make a mess of things, although, at the moment, I really didn't think she would welcome that at all.

As I walked, I thought of our stepbrother, Michael, and our first meeting. He'd come to the house, where Mum had prepared a fantastic tea, spread out across the dining room table like a banquet. I'd been prepared to dislike him, sick of the fuss that was being made and the feeling that Rose and I were being relegated to second best just because this wonderful man had turned up out of the blue. But I couldn't because he was nice, really nice, chatty and affectionate — wow, he gave me a bear hug as soon as he saw me, for God's sake. He smelled good too, sort of citrusy, a scent that clung to his clothes and his dark hair, cropped short, and at the tender age of only twenty-nine, flecked with grey at the temples.

I tried to see Mum in his looks, but there was nothing,

not even eye color. Mum's were a deep brown, but his were hazel green with yellow flecks like a cat that glowed brightly when the sun hit them. He was stocky, broad-chested, muscular with large hands and thick fingers, with clean short square nails. He had a flat open face with a smudge of a nose and a smile that could break your heart. The perfect boy next door. I wasn't surprised that Mum and Rose were smitten. I think I would be, too…eventually.

Apparently, he'd worked as a reporter for a local Swansea newspaper. He wrote under the by-line "Michael Fisher — Fishing for News," and commented on new up-and-coming bands, wrote detailed reviews of local gigs, and printed real-life stories about new authors, singers, and songwriters. Hey, maybe he'd have an interest in Blake and his new wannabe band. Connections, that's all it amounted to, really. Oh, and talent, of course! All his work was featured in a weekly pull-out called "The Gig."

I let myself in the back door when I got home, which opened straight into the kitchen. The room was empty, although I noticed that something smelling pretty good was baking in the oven. "Hello, anyone around?"

I walked into the hallway and, dumping my bag on the floor, hung my jacket on the coat stand.

"Yes, Ruby, in here." Mum's voice, sounding slightly panicked, was coming from the conservatory. I had to walk through the dining room to get there, which, to my surprise, smelled strongly of cigarette smoke. Nobody in the house smoked, so this was really weird. Did I imagine it? Mum, sitting on one of the comfortable cane chairs, discreetly batting the air with her hands, a tell-tale wreath of smoke coiling above her head, smiled brightly and said, "Hi, Ruby. How was school today?"

I stood in the doorway and gave an exaggerated sniff. "Mum?"

"What?" she said, looking all around like she'd lost something. Then, after a hasty glance at me, she realized she had to come clean and shamefacedly said, "Okay. I've had a cigarette. Please don't tell Dad, will you? You know what he's like about smoking."

She looked so much like a little girl caught in mischief that I had to smile. "No, I won't tell Dad. Where is he anyway?"

"It's Wednesday — late night at the surgery."

"Oh yeah, of course. Why are you smoking, though, Mum? What's wrong?"

I sat down on the cane chair opposite her. Sunshine fell in golden pools on the tiled floor through the massive arched conservatory windows, and in the garden, bees and bright colored butterflies circled the massive buddleia bush. The garden was a beautiful blaze of emerald, red, orange, and gold.

"Oh, you know, I suppose I feel a little stressed, with Michael turning up and…. Oh, I don't know, Ruby." She hung her head and raked a hand through her hair.

"Where's Rose?" I asked her gently.

"Gone for a walk with Michael." She must have seen the hurt look on my face that they'd gone off together without asking me because she said quickly, "Oh, I'm sure she'd have asked you if you'd been here, but she knows you have your walk home from school every day. Michael asked about you, though."

"Mum, Rose barely speaks to me now since I got back from France. Not even at work."

"I know, I have noticed, Ruby. She was upset at you going off alone the way you did, and she's so stubborn. You two have always been so different from each other."

"I had to go off like that, Mum. Rose wouldn't have let me go alone. She would have followed me — you know that."

Reluctantly Mum nodded. "I've barely spoken to you either. I've been so distracted. Tell me more about your holiday. Did you meet any nice people?"

I frowned and said, "Has Dad said anything to you?"

She shook her head no but then said, "Why? Should he have?"

This time it was my turn to shake my head before saying, "I'll come back to that. There's something I need to ask you first."

She looked at me expectantly.

"Mum, how do you know that Michael is your son?"

"I just know. Believe me, Ruby, Michael is my son and your half brother, and obviously Rose's half brother too."

"Yes, but how do you know for absolute sure? He could be anybody. Have you had one of those tests, DNA tests?"

"I don't need to," she replied. There was a short silence before Mum said, "Ruby, Michael looks exactly like his dad."

"So you've seen Michael's dad recently?" I asked in surprise.

"Yes," said Mum.

"I don't understand." And when she didn't reply, I pressed further. "Mum...?"

"Let's go and make a cuppa," she said, rising slowly to

her feet and holding out her hand for mine. "And then I'll tell you everything. Oh, and while we're having a heart-to-heart, I want to know what happened about the library job. I'm sure there's more to that than meets the eye."

She nodded knowingly as I cowered under the unwavering stare from her dark eyes. "Well," I began to say. "I don't like to tell on Rose, but...."

She smiled and gave me a wink.

Chapter Seven

It had been four days since I'd heard from Blake, four whole days since I'd sent the text asking about his meeting with the possible band members. I also told him that I missed him and hoped to see him very soon. He hadn't replied to my jokey text about Jim Morrison and the maracas, that being the reason I'd texted again. Okay, four days wasn't that long, I supposed, but because we'd been in touch a lot, I was getting worried.

Visions of him being in some sort of trouble flashed through my mind. Had he been kidnapped by some dodgy French gang who was after—I don't know—his guitar? Fallen over in the street and banged his head? Been involved in a car accident? Or, horror of horrors—worst thing of all—had he gone off with another woman? I felt distinctly down and dispirited, and the only thing I seemed able to do was to sit there on my bed and gaze at my phone, waiting impatiently for a message to pop up.

How frustrating that text messaging or possibly ringing was our only contact. I had no email for him and no actual address, although I could possibly contact the B&B he'd been staying in if I could remember what it was called. We'd been so caught up with La Petite Amelia and La Bar as meeting places that nothing else had seemed to matter. With a sense of relief, I realized I could contact La Bar if I really needed to. My mind was all over the place—how lucky that it was Saturday and I didn't have to work.

My phone beeped, and looking at it straight away, desperate for it to be a message from Blake, I saw that, yeah, it was a message…but from James! I read it curiously. I'd never had a text from James before, and of course, I hadn't got in touch with him while I was away, so I could only think that he'd got my number from Rose.

Hey Ruby, hope u okay and enjoyed your trip to France. Don't forget the gang's night out tonight cos of firework night. 8.00 pm in the Bluebell. Will be good to have a catch up. Seems ages since we spoke J xxx

By the gang, I assumed he meant me, Rose, Vanessa, Steve, Craig, and, of course, James. All purely friends. None of us were couples. I'd known nothing about it. Obviously Rose hadn't invited me but, thinking about it, why shouldn't I go? James had asked me to, and I had more right to be there than Rose did, really, considering that Vanessa was my friend first from college. Okay, we'd both known the boys since school, but I'd invited Rose along the first time we'd all met up, just to make it an even number really, and also because, at that time, Rose and I went everywhere together. Oh, happy days.

I felt quite buoyed up and excited about a night out. After

all, I hadn't been out to a bar for a drink since being in France with Blake. That, of course, encouraged all sorts of worrying things to flit through my mind, and, gazing longingly at my phone, I wished it would beep, and a reassuring message pop up. Also, though, I hadn't been out with the usual gang to the local pubs in Emsworth for ages, weeks before I went away. I'd been bored with it but now felt that a night out would do me good, and it would be great to catch up with James.

The bedroom door opened and peering over the top of the room divider, I was pleased to see it was Rose. She looked good in a pair of skinny jeans and a long red T-shirt, the words, I Love Music With Soul, written across the front in loopy white letters, which immediately made me think of Blake and his comment about today's music having no soul. I had the exact same T-shirt hanging in the wardrobe.

"Hey, Rose."

She looked up in alarm. "God, Ruby. You made me jump. I thought you'd be out walking. It's Saturday...."

"I'm going out soon, but...." Just having a response from her and hearing her voice made me really tempted to confide in her about Blake. At one time, we would have discussed it in depth for hours and gone through, and even written a list of the pros and cons of hearing from him or not hearing from him. The thought that we didn't do that now made me sad.

She gazed at me questioningly, yet not quite meeting my eye. "But what?"

"Oh, nothing. Just that James texted me, so I know about tonight, about meeting in the Bluebell. Just thought I might go."

"Okay." She shrugged as if she couldn't care one way or another and then flounced herself down full length on the bed and began to study her phone as if it was the most interesting thing in the world. "I'm thinking of having a little sleep," she told me. "So don't slam the door on your way out."

"Rose, can we talk?"

"No, not at the moment," she replied sulkily. She put her phone on the bedside cabinet and turned on her side, away from me. "I'm tired, couldn't sleep last night."

A sense of elation crept through me at the fact that Rose was at least willing to talk, so, picking up my rucksack and shrugging on my coat, I said cheerfully, "Okay, tonight then."

She pretended to fall asleep really quickly, her breathing long and exaggerated, but I knew she hadn't, and that she watched me through half-closed eyelids as I went out and gently closed the door.

Mum and Dad were busy in the garden, cutting and mowing and sweeping colorful leaves into piles. I shivered in the chilly air, hunching my shoulders, pulling on my gloves, and watching as a strengthening breeze chased the leaves around the garden, making it virtually impossible for Dad to collect them all and put them in his big green garden waste bag. Mum, giggling hysterically at his antics, looked young and happy and decidedly more positive than she had the other day. Maybe our good long talk had done her good. With a cheery wave, I set off out the garden gate and headed down the High Street. Maybe I'd call in at the bakers Smith & Vosper on the way. They did a really yummy vegetable pasty.

I checked my phone as I came to the shops, hoping to

see a text message from Blake, but there was nothing. The awful thought that he was ignoring me flashed through my mind, and my stomach churned. No, surely not—Blake wouldn't do that. He was far too upfront and truthful, and I was pretty sure if he had found somebody else, he would tell me. Wouldn't he? Hmm, maybe not.

There was only one thing for it. I couldn't keep sending text after text, so later, when the time was right, when I was totally alone on the seashore, I would ring him and find out exactly what was going on. No excuses. I had to know the truth about the awful long silence he was putting me through. I felt suddenly strong and empowered as I strode down the slippery cobbled street.

An unusually strong smell of incense, mixing with the odor of bacon sandwiches and baking pastry, wreathed its way through the air, bringing to my attention that a new shop had opened up a couple of doors away from the baker's. I stopped to admire the jewelry displayed in the window. Beautiful long silver chains draped across little red satin cushions, earrings hanging from little trees and rings in sumptuous boxes set with twinkling diamonds, rubies, and emeralds. Whether or not the stones were real at such a cheap price, I wasn't sure, but whatever, they looked pretty good to me. The shop also sold things like joss sticks, scented candles, tarot cards, spiritual healing and self-help books. I didn't remember ever seeing a shop like this in Emsworth. It would be interesting to see how it fared.

I was just about to walk on when I spotted a little handwritten poster in the window advertising tarot readings and palm readings by Joanna—introductory offer ten pounds for thirty minutes instead of the usual twenty pounds. Come on in, and let me tell you your future! Normally I scorned this type of thing. How could anybody predict your future with a pack of cards or know what was going to happen to you from the lines on your hands? Ridiculous. But, I don't know, maybe because I was worried at not hearing from Blake and was desperate to know what was going to happen, I found myself walking into the shop, going straight to the counter, and asking for Joanna.

~*~

Later, sitting at home, my mind returned to the conversation I'd had with Mum. I remembered her blowing on her tea, her breath mixing with the spiraling steam, before taking a sip, grimacing as the hot brew burned her tongue. The tea pot, sugar bowl, and milk jug stood close by on the table. Mum loved her tea. We'd decided to stay in the kitchen, so I took off my coat and hung it over the back of the chair before sitting down opposite her. Gulping at my creamy hot chocolate — I didn't like tea. Even the smell of it made me cringe — my hands wrapped around the mug, I inhaled the lovely smell coming from whatever was still baking in the oven. I noticed that Mum looked tired, the lines on either side of her mouth deep grooves, and the skin beneath her eyes yellow and thin as paper.

"Chicken pie," said Mum as if reading my mind, and then, "Okay then, tell me all about the library job."

"Hey, that's not fair, Mum. You said you'd tell me all about Michael and his dad first of all."

Mum looked slightly shamefaced and, taking a deep breath, said, "Well, I've seen Michael's dad over the years.

We always kept in touch because…. Well, Michael is his baby too, and okay, he was taken straight away, but at least I saw him, I had a glimpse. Nick never did—"

"Nick?"

"Yes, he's called Nick Peters. Look, I'm going to be very truthful here. Whatever you might think of me, even though we were so young at the time, Ruby, we loved each other. If we'd been older, if things had been different, we would have had the baby and gotten married."

"Wow. I didn't realize…. What does this mean, though, Mum? What about Dad?"

Mum frowned. "This has nothing to do with my feelings for your dad. I met dad a long time after all that happened. Nick and I had moved on and—well, I couldn't stay with him, not without our baby. Good God, Ruby, I care about your dad very much. I have a very good life with him. After all the years together, we're still good friends."

A question that I knew I shouldn't ask hovered tantalizingly on my tongue. I took another sip of hot chocolate before saying quietly, "Have you been unfaithful with Nick Peters, Mum?"

"No." Mum shook her head and then repeated firmly, "No. Not physically, anyway." I frowned and looked at her questioningly, sipping at my drink. "Maybe mentally. Sometimes after we've met and talked for an hour or two… well, I miss him and think about him for a long time after."

"Is he married?"

"Yes. He lives in Horndean with his wife, Julie, and has two daughters, Lisa and Gemma. I think they're twenty-eight and twenty-nine, just a little older than you and Rose."

Mum looked up and gazed at me, an expression on her face that I'd never seen before. The sort of look that said this is the total truth, and you'll just have to take it.

"Tell me about the day Michael turned up. What happened?"

"Well, it was weird," she told me. "And really, I'm still reeling from the shock." She was warming to our talk and poured more tea, adding a splash of milk and so few grains of sugar it was hardly worth it. "I was alone in the house, which I was glad about when I thought about everything later. It would have been awful if your dad had been home. Anyway, I heard a knock on the front door. I was hoping it was a delivery from Amazon. I'd ordered a book that I was really looking forward to reading, so I rushed to the door, opened it, and bam, there he was, just standing there." She gazed into the middle distance as if she had forgotten I was there but was strongly reliving what had happened that day. "And Ruby...." She looked at me fully now. "Do you know what? I knew it was him. I knew it was my Michael. Even though it had been such a long time, and I hadn't seen him since he was a newborn baby, I knew it was him."

I nodded my head. "Go on," I urged. "What happened next?"

"'Mum?' he said, and I said, 'Michael?' Well, he crushed me in a massive hug until I could barely breathe and kept saying, 'Mum, Mum! I've found you. I've found you!' I had never thought I'd ever see him again. My mum had to wrench him from my arms that day as I sat in my hospital bed. I really didn't want to give him up. I really didn't think I'd feel that way, but I made the decision to do it with Nan and Grandad."

Tears started to well up in her eyes. She tried to stop them with a finger, but they trickled slowly down her cheeks. I dug around in my coat pockets and brought out a packet from which I peeled a tissue and thrust it into her hand.

"Thank you, Ruby," she said, sniffing hard, then blowing her nose and dabbing at her wet cheeks. The now damp tissue shredded in her fingers, and little white bits fell onto the table like flakes of snow. "When I finally got with your dad," she told me as she tried to gulp back tears, "I couldn't bring myself to marry him for years, even though he'd asked me to, because — this will probably sound stupid to you, Ruby — but I felt disrespectful to Michael. I couldn't see how I could ever get married and have other children because it wouldn't be fair to him. How could I give birth to and keep other children if I couldn't keep him?"

Slowly I shook my head. "No, that doesn't sound stupid, Mum. I understand. I can relate to that, as I'm sure most people could." I snaked my hand across the table and clasped hers.

She smiled and, nodding towards our entwined hands, said wistfully, "My hands used to look like yours, smooth and white with no wrinkles and lines. Look at them now."

"Hey, Mum," I said with a giggle. "They're not bad for a fifty some year old." There was a short pause, just the sound of Mum sniffing and blowing her nose, before I said, "Do you think Nan and Grandad would like to meet Michael?"

"I'm not sure," she replied. "I don't know whether or not to tell them about him yet. To tell you the truth, Ruby, I don't want to dredge up bad memories. I know they've regretted the decision over the years, just as I have. I just don't know." There was a short silence before she said, "Oh Ruby, I was such a silly young girl."

"No, Mum," I reassured her, shaking my head. "You weren't. You fell in love; that was all."

Sniffing hard again, she blew her nose and then poured more tea while saying, "Well come on, Ruby, quickly, before Rose and Michael get back. Tell me everything about the library job. And," she fixed me with a hard stare, "About your holiday too. I feel there's been something on your mind since you came back."

Taking a deep breath, I unburdened myself, as it were, and told Mum everything.

Chapter Eight

The Bluebell was heaving, thirsty crowds pushing and shoving against each other four deep at the bar, and the staff, hot and sweaty, was rushing around in a panic. I'd walked to the pub with Rose and Vanessa and thank God for Vanessa, who had chattered away non-stop, masking the fact that Rose was still barely speaking to me. I was hoping that a drink or two would loosen her up so we could have that talk I'd mentioned earlier. I noticed that even though we hadn't intentionally copied each other, we both wore skinny jeans with knee-high boots and silky black shirts, silver chains dangling around our necks.

As it was firework night, there was a turn on, as my dad always said, and the music was good, a mixture of Bob Dylan, the Byrds, the Doors, Rod Stewart, and the Beatles. Older music, music with soul. It reminded me so much of Blake that I felt a lump in my throat and thought I might cry. I fervently hoped he didn't play the Stones, especially "Ruby

Tuesday." There was no way I could cope with that song at the moment. Even the singer reminded me of Blake, an older hippy guy, strumming on a guitar. He wore jeans, a black waistcoat over a white open-necked shirt, and a trilby tilted at a cool angle on his head.

I'd still not heard from him, not a single text message, and when I'd rung his phone from a secluded place on the shore, nobody around but the squawking gulls, the phone had simply rung and rung and rung before abruptly cutting off. There was no disembodied voice telling me to try again later, so no way of leaving a message. I supposed I could ring again and maybe send one more text message, but if Blake had decided to cut contact, then I supposed I'd have to go along with it, however much it hurt.

The tarot reader I'd seen that afternoon came to mind, and a sudden dart of what could only be termed hope pierced my heart as I thought of what she'd said. Things that she had no way of knowing. She talked of a holiday romance which would become so much more than that, of a choice I would have to make, "between two lovers." Yes, those were her exact words. *Huh*, I thought. *I haven't even got one lover, let alone two!*

When she'd finished with the cards, she read my palms, inspecting them carefully and tracing the lines with her long pointy nails. She exclaimed over the length of my lifeline and, studying carefully, announced that someday I would have two children, a boy and a girl—What?—and that, "although things look pretty bleak at the moment" and "you think you've lost your love" that wasn't the case at all. She then told me the job I wanted was there and mine for the taking, and then surprisingly, said. "I feel it should have been yours in the first place." She looked at me expectantly, but I wasn't about to give anything away, so I kept my mouth firmly closed, lips pursed together.

"Keep hopeful and brave," she told me as I put a ten-pound note into her outstretched hand. "Your life is blessed, Ruby Tuesday." It was only when I'd left the shop and was on my walk, crunching along the shore, that I realized with a feeling of total shock that I hadn't even told her my name. And yet.... I must have told her. A weird shiver ran down my spine.

A nudge from Vanessa brought me back to earth and, moving away from the bar, we managed to find a table. It hadn't been cleared and was festooned with sticky glasses, some with suspect-looking dregs in the bottom, which, gingerly holding them with the tips of our fingers, we took to the bar. Sitting down, we sipped our drinks, peering over the top of the crowd for a glimpse of the act, nodding our heads and tapping our feet to the music.

James grinned, and leaning closer, said, "He's good," nodding his head towards the singer. I nodded my agreement. James looked smart wearing black trousers, a cream open-necked shirt, and a black casual jacket. A group of women at the next table, all dressed up as if on a hen night, suddenly shrieked really loudly.

"How was your holiday?" he asked.

I could barely hear him because of the sheer volume of noise but said, "Really good."

He gave a slight nod towards Rose. "Is she speaking to you yet?"

I shrugged and said, "Perhaps later. I intend to have a

talk with her."

"She was mad at you going away without telling her."

A group of young men whooping it up with the hen party was encouraging the ladies to act even wilder and noisier, so I leaned in closer to James, the citrusy scent of his cologne heady and intoxicating. "I had no choice, James. I needed some time to myself."

"If it makes any difference," he whispered, so close that his breath tickled my ear, "I missed you, Ruby. And if you ever have time for that drink, just the two of us…?"

The music suddenly stopped, and James's words, unnaturally loud, hovered in the air. People turned to stare and grin, and James, pink with embarrassment, smiled like a child as Craig and Steve got up to get more drinks. The hippy singer was taking a well-earned break and sipping thirstily from a foaming pint, when to my utter astonishment, Rose raised her glass to me and said, "Are you having another, Ruby?"

We sat outside then, huddled into our identical coats, where the air was fresh and damp, and fallen leaves glowed on the paths like hot coals. The acrid smell of bonfires and fireworks, mixed with salt from the sea, hung in the air, and the drink from Rose slipped warm and oily down my throat. The sky arched overhead, dark as pitch and sparkling with stars and the great globe of the moon. We talked then, arm in arm, heads close together, lit by a yellow light that pooled onto the pavement from the windows of the pub. Friends again. Rose, my twin, the other side of me, the other half of my face.

The rest of the gang stayed inside, leaving us to talk.

The music started again, the singer's raspy voice doing a great cover of "Maggie May." She told me she'd been hurt when I went off alone but listened carefully when I explained how I felt, that I needed to be just me for a while, without my twin. I'm not sure she understood fully. Rose liked being a twin. She liked the attention we got when we were together, how people exclaimed at our likeness, our cuteness, and thought it great that we wore the same clothes. She nodded, though, and agreed and squeezed my hand, saying she thought it had been her getting the library job that had upset me. She'd beaten herself up about it and regretted what she'd done.

"I was so selfish," she said. "You should have said no — the job should have been yours. I was unhappy about the money as well," stated Rose.

"Money?" I asked.

"We're supposed to be saving for a deposit on a place together. We'll never move from Mum and Dad's if we don't do that, Ruby."

"Money that I save each month still went into the pot," I told her. "My holiday made no difference to that. I still want us to get a place together. Do you?"

"Yes, of course, I do."

We talked about Michael and the fact that Rose had asked him to join us that evening, but he'd said he couldn't, that he had something he needed to deal with. Something important.

"Now, what was all that about?" she said. "What has Michael to deal with that he can't tell us about?"

"You've only just met him, Rose," I told her, "There could be anything going on in his life, not only us."

"But he's just found Mum," she protested. "What else could be more important than that?"

I shook my head. Rose could be so trying at times. Michael could have all sorts of things going on in his life. He didn't have to tell us everything. "Has he got a partner?" I asked her. "Maybe he's got a wife he hasn't told us about?"

She shook her head and shrugged. "Maybe, but he hasn't said anything. Surely he would have told Mum if he had a wife." Glancing at the pub next door, the Coal Exchange where Michael was staying, she said, "We'll call in there. He'll surely turn up later."

Vanessa came outside, followed closely by Steve, Craig, and James, attracting a lot of attention because of her short clingy skirt wriggling up her thighs like worms. The Coal Exchange was quieter than the Bluebell. There was no live music, just a jukebox playing softly. Some of the tables were taken by groups of chattering people, some eating the specialty pizza and dipping into deep bowls of well-browned chips. A few old men were hunched at the bar clutching their pints.

The landlord, Robert, served us, a powerful-looking man with muscular arms—it must be because of the hand-pulled pumps—who, for some strange reason, sported an old-fashioned handlebar moustache, putting me in mind of a cyclist or a weight lifter from the nineteen twenties. He began to pour pints from the many hand pumps lined up along the bar. I noticed that the guys were having ESB, extra-strong bitter, while we three girls opted for wine. The pub was pleasantly blurry to my intoxicated brain, which was why I suppose that I didn't take much notice of what Robert said at first.

"Hey, you two look-a-likes. What's happened to Michael?" He was innocent of the background story to Michael but knew he had a connection with me and Rose — or the two look-a-likes, as he always called us. "He hasn't been here for a couple of days, and...." He leaned across the pumps and lowered his voice to a whisper. "He hasn't paid his bill."

"Really?" said Rose. "He came to our house yesterday. I thought he was still staying here."

Robert shook his head. "Nope. Not seen him since day before yesterday. I've not a clue what to do about the room. I rang his mobile, but the number I've got is a no number."

"Well, he is a naughty boy," said Vanessa, draping herself over the bar like a tea towel drying on a beer pump and wagging a wayward finger.

Everybody laughed except Robert, who, although smiling, gave her a stern warning. "Oy, no tipsiness in here, Vanessa." Which was a pretty stupid thing to say, as we were in a pub. Robert was well known for his own teetotalism, probably brought on by his mum and dad's notorious drunk and disorderly conduct around Emsworth. I noticed with a smile that Craig put a proprietorial arm around Vanessa's waist and pulled her close.

"I'll contact him tomorrow," said Rose, taking charge. "We need to find out what's going on here, don't we, Ruby?"

I nodded while Robert said, "Yeah, please, if you could. I have to know if I can re-let the room, and...," He raised his eyebrows, "I need my money. I've got bills to pay, you know."

We left the pub in a haze, Rose hanging on my arm like a handbag, a fleeting kiss on the cheek from James as we said goodnight, and then suddenly it was the next morning, and I awoke to a thin burst of sunlight pouring through the windows. Trees swaying violently in a strong wind shed their leaves in a crimson and gold blur. A sick headache thumped across my brow and Rose, snoring heavily behind the room divider, mumbled in her sleep as I turned onto my side and tried to doze off again.

~*~

Breakfast was a dismal affair, brought on, of course, by the news we had to give Mum and Dad about Michael not having been at the pub for a couple of days. "It's only what Robert said last night," Rose assured them. "He could have turned up by now and be safely asleep in his bed in the Coal Exchange." She picked and poked at some frothy-looking scrambled eggs. The kitchen smelled stuffy with warmth and frying, and a strong wind howled around the house like ghosts.

"When did you last hear from him, Mum?" I asked.

She looked into space, thinking, pulling her robe around her as if she was cold. "A couple of days ago," she replied. "Umm, he texted…what's today, Sunday? He texted on Thursday and said he would be in touch at the weekend. I thought we might see him today."

Dad carried on eating, cutting hungrily through the bacon, eggs, and mushrooms arranged as neatly as a still life painting on his plate, spreading thick slices of toast with butter and strawberry jam. He took a sip of coffee, dark enough to be called black, and said, "Hmm."

"Is that all you can say, Stan?" asked Mum. "My long-lost son has disappeared from my life again, and all you can say is 'hmm'?"

"May," replied Dad, glancing at her, his eyes a piercing blue, while calmly making an egg sandwich with leftover toast. "He'll turn up again when he's ready. We should leave him to it." Egg yolk ran down his chin in a yellow river as he munched heartily.

"Chin, Dad," said Rose, patting her own chin with an outstretched finger.

"I'll ring him," said Mum defiantly, reaching for her phone and scrolling down to find the number. She mumbled to herself, "I can't understand this. Michael isn't like that. He wouldn't just disappear." Rose and I waited with bated breath, watching the hopeful expression on Mum's face. I scooped milk and cereal with a spoon and chewed thoughtfully, and then sipped orange juice, the taste cold and tangy in my parched mouth.

"It's ringing," said Mum. It rang for a while before, with evident disappointment, she hung up and placed the phone carefully on the table. "I'll try again later," she said.

"I could text," offered Rose, "If you want me to."

Mum nodded okay, and Rose began tip-tapping with her long nails onto the keypad. "Okay, I've just said, *Hi, hope you're okay. Please get in touch. Would be good to meet up again.*"

She looked around the table expectantly. Mum nodded, and Dad said while adding sugar to his coffee and stirring it quickly, "Yes, then all we can do is wait for him to contact us." He patted Mum's hand with his fingers and gave her a small smile. "We could always pop into the Coal Exchange for lunch, have a look around. Maybe he'll have turned up, and we can talk to him."

Tears welled into her eyes, and jumping up, I tore off a piece of kitchen roll and handed it to her. "Lunch?" she said, sniffing hard. "With all that you've eaten now, you won't be hungry at supper, let alone lunch!"

Despite Dad's laughter at Mum's comment, I knew they were both worried, and I hoped fervently that nothing bad had happened to Michael. What was going on, though? I'd checked my phone this morning, and still nothing from Blake either. Had all lines of communication disappeared? I had an awful feeling now that I'd been played, that he'd had no intention of contacting me and had disappeared, never to be seen again.

He was probably already with somebody else. Another girl that had turned up in St. Malo just as I had. Somebody new and green, somebody who, just as I had, would believe every word he said. Somebody else he could serenade with silly love songs. My heart ached so badly, I had to take long, deep breaths to steady myself.

I prayed that he would turn up eventually. After all, I knew everything about him. I knew he was a Londoner born in the West End and that his mum was called Elaine and his dad Alf. His mum worked as a legal secretary—just like my mum, but in probate and not conveyancing—and his dad was a taxi driver—he drove those lovely big black London cabs. He had a younger brother, Will, who wanted to be a famous musician just as Blake did, but for the moment, he played in a local band in the West End pubs and clubs. I knew he loved thick black coffee and croissants for breakfast and that he loved to vape but really wanted to be able to smoke proper cigarettes without ruining his health. Oh, and he loved to run and to work out with weights but didn't get a lot of time for that because his music came first.

All this flashed through my mind as, glancing at Mum, I wondered how she really felt about Michael now. Why had he done it? Why had he turned up out of the blue, made Mum so happy, and then disappeared, never to be seen again? Hold on a minute, though. Maybe I was jumping the gun. How did we know he wasn't going to reappear? He'd seemed so nice, so genuine. No, I couldn't believe for a moment that he wouldn't turn up again.

"Well, okay, maybe not lunch," stated Dad. "If he doesn't get in touch by tomorrow, I'll go pay his bill at the pub and then we'll investigate."

"Investigate?" Mum, Rose, and I said at exactly the same time, and then giggled because we couldn't believe it just happened.

"Hmm," said Dad nodding his head.

"Stan, don't keep saying hmm," said Mum irritably. "If you know something, then spit it out."

"I don't know anything," replied Dad. "But he did mention a lady he knows who lives in Bosham."

"A lady in Bosham?" asked Mum, scandalized. "He didn't mention a lady to me."

"Don't worry, May," assured Dad. "We'll find him." He stood up and began to amble slowly from the room. He stopped in the doorway and said, as if an afterthought said, "Oh, by the way, you two girls, glad you're on speaking terms again."

Rose gave me a sidelong glance. "Yeah, I finally came to my senses."

"Stan," Mum shouted indignantly. "Surely you're going to help with the dishes?"

"Back in a minute, dear," he shouted back.

Rose and I exchanged a wry glance while Mum looked at her phone yet again. "No call back from Michael yet," she informed us in a flat empty voice.

Chapter Nine

The house looked empty, abandoned, its windows like sightless eyes. I felt a tiny surge of annoyance at the state of the place — after all, it had so much going for it. It was in Bosham, for God's sake, a fabulous place. The harbor was just a short walk away, and there was an ancient church, restaurants, shops, and sailing clubs. It was surrounded by other massive houses — massive, *well-kept* houses, though — set in a fantastic large mature garden, with lots of trees and bushes and grass. Okay, any flowers had died by now, but in the spring and summer, I'd no doubt it would have looked pretty good.

Mum, Dad, me, and Rose had come to investigate after finding out some interesting information from Robert at the pub. After waiting a few days with still no sign of Michael, Dad and I had gone to the Coal Exchange, paid Michael's bill and, after a very enlightening conversation with Robert, had come home with the address that Michael had checked in with. And it definitely wasn't an address in Swansea.

"Yeah," said Robert, looking intently at the bookings on his laptop. "He used 3 Larchwood Avenue, Bosham as his check-in address. Bear in mind, though, this could be a wrong address. I mean, he has given me a dodgy phone number."

Frowning, Dad checked the phone number for Michael that he had on his mobile, and peering at the screen of Robert's computer, said, "No, you've got it wrong, Robert. That's a two and a three, not two twos."

"Aah, okay, I'll change that." He fiddled with the mouse, and using the keyboard, began deleting numbers and putting new ones in. "I stand corrected."

"Even so," Dad said, "He's not picking up anyway. May has rung him hundreds of times. In fact, if I was Michael, I'd report her as a stalker." He gave a short bark of laughter, to which Robert joined in, attracting the languid attention of a couple of lunchtime drinkers sitting at the bar.

"Hmm, I think this calls for a visit to Bosham, don't you, Ruby?"

I nodded, and Robert said, "Yeah, if the address exists."

"I don't understand," said Dad as we finally left the pub. "Why didn't he tell us he had a house so close by, in Bosham? And why was he living at the pub? It doesn't make sense."

"I don't know, Dad," I replied. "Maybe if we go to the house, we'll get some answers. Maybe the house belongs to the 'lady from Bosham' that was mentioned before."

Dad nodded and frowned. "Good point, Ruby. Just wait until your mum knows about this."

Well, Robert, I thought as, a few hours later, we stood in the garden of 3 Larchwood Avenue. *The address certainly does exist, but where is Michael?*

"Wow," said Dad, gazing at the house, his hands on his hips. "This place must be worth a fortune." He shook his head as if baffled that Michael could have afforded to buy such a place on a salary as a reporter for a local newspaper.

Rose was already at the sitting-room window, peering through, her hands cupped around her face. "It's more or less empty," she said. "Only a dodgy-looking three-piece suite with holes in it and the stuffing spewing out. Even bare floorboards — or maybe they're supposed to be like that? Oh, and a picture on the wall." She peered intently. "A black and white photo of a woman holding a child, a little girl."

"I wonder who she is?" said Mum, joining Rose at the window, looking through the glass intently like a burglar in training.

"His girlfriend? His wife?" mused Rose.

"Well," I said, "Whoever she is, she's very pretty." She had long black hair with a fringe cut straight across, skimming her eyebrows and emphasizing her slanty eyes. The little girl was dark too, with great luminous eyes set beneath high cheekbones. Eyes that seemed to follow you wherever you went. Something about her features, the nose and the mouth, reminded me of Michael, and the certainty that she was Michael's daughter flitted into my mind. Oh my God, Mum's granddaughter.

"She looks like Cher back in the day," commented Mum of the woman.

"'I got you, babe,'" crooned Dad, coming up behind Mum and sneaking his arms around her waist.

Mum jumped and shrieked, "Stan!" as he bellowed

with laughter.

"Ssh," whispered me and Rose together, putting a finger to our lips. "Somebody might be in —"

"Yeah," said Dad sarcastically. "That's sort of what we're hoping, isn't it? You know, why we're here — really?"

We all ignored him as we crept around to the back of the house and peeked into what was obviously the dining room. A long shiny wooden table stood in the middle of the room, flanked by four chairs, and a large earthenware vase filled with dried grasses stood solitary in a corner. The kitchen was clean and tidy but sparse, just a bright pink kettle on the work top with a jar of instant coffee and an open bag of sugar, around which a few granules sparkled in the meager light falling through the window. A packet of biscuits, crisps, and a couple of cans of beer stood nearby.

"Somebody's been in there recently," said Dad, nodding towards the coffee and the sugar, the little pile of provisions. "And a bright pink kettle? It's got to be a woman, hasn't it?"

"Sexist!" groaned Mum.

"Men love pink these days, don't ya know," pointed out Rose in a silly voice.

Dad tried the back door handle, but it was locked, and then we noticed that the long narrow window next to the door had a broken window pane. Dad snaked his hand in, careful to avoid the jagged edges of the glass, but there was no key in the lock. "That's how he got in," said Dad. "I wonder if he's in there now." Without missing a beat, he bellowed, "Michael, come on out. We're here to help you."

Mum, her hands to her crimson cheeks, said, "Stan,

ssh! You'll have the neighbors out! And anyway, Michael might not be in there."

"Oh, and who exactly do you think is in there?" asked Dad, giving her a sideways glance. "A bevy of women protecting their 'pink kettle'?"

"Ha ha, very funny, Stan. No, anyone could be in there. Um…squatters," she suggested quickly.

Dad gave a wry smile and shouted for Michael again. "We need some action around here, May. We need to know what's going on with him. If the neighbors do hear us…. Well, they may be able to help. If there are squatters, they're in trouble!"

I shivered and hunched into my coat, pulling my beanie tighter on my head and my gloves tighter on my hands. The last of the leaves rustled on the trees and fell slowly to the ground, bulking the crispy carpet underfoot. Tiny raindrops spat at the ground, and, for warmth, I suppose, Rose too hunched her shoulders to her ears and clung to my arm.

We did another circuit of the whole house and grounds, spying in the windows, tapping on the doors. Dad tried putting his hand through the hole in the window again, but this time attempted to unlock the door with a length of silver wire that he just happened to have in his pocket. "A little trick I learned in the army," he told us with a wink, but still no luck. Dad had done a very short stint in the services when he was young.

"Fat lot of good that little trick did you, eh?" remarked Mum sarcastically.

We tramped over the grass so many times that leaves of gold and crimson and orange stuck to our boots and raindrops, heavy now and persistent, soaked into our coats and our hats.

"One last time," said Dad before bellowing again like an angry bull, but there was nothing, no response whatsoever, not even from the neighbors. No twitching curtains or opening of doors, and no indignant person standing on their front step wondering who was making all the noise. Full of disappointment, we wandered out to the car, Mum's eyes watering again, and began to clamber in. Mum was in the front, Rose and I in the back when we heard a voice, shrill and panicky.

"No, wait! Mum, wait!"

And there he was, Michael, bearing a close resemblance to one of the old homeless men I'd seen sleeping rough in the doorway of the Scope Charity shop on Emsworth High Street. He'd outgrown his designer stubble, which was now a thick bushy beard coating most of his face and chin. He wore grubby jeans and a pale blue jumper, threadbare at the elbows and neckline, and as he ran towards us across the sodden grass, I noticed that his feet were bare. What on earth had happened to the handsome boy next door?

"Oh, Michael," said Mum, getting out of the car and opening her arms to him. "Whatever is the matter?" Dad peered at them from the driver's seat. I saw that his knuckles were taut and white as his hands clutched hard at the steering wheel. Rose made to get out of the car, but I held her back with my arm.

"She's gone, Mum," he sobbed. "She's gone...and taken Leah. I'll never see her again. I know I won't."

He wept, such a sad sound, tearing at our hearts as

they stood so close, his forehead on Mum's shoulder, her chin on Michael's neck, one body, two heads, just like conjoined twins.

~*~

I stood at the window in mine and Rose's bedroom staring at the garden, which looked changed somehow, subtly altered, by a thin dusting of snow. It coated the path and the lawn and the flower beds like sweet, creamy icing on a wedding cake. Trees stood still as statues, their twisted branches glowing white against the landscape. Tiny flakes blew crazily in a stiff cold breeze, splattering against the window and staying for a moment pressed to the glass in the intricate patterns of a kaleidoscope. The heat of the radiator against my legs felt too comforting, too warm, making it all but impossible to go outside. I moved slightly away.

"You're surely not going walking today, are you, Ruby?" came Rose's sleepy voice from behind the divider. "The BBC weather report says it's snowing out."

"There's only a dusting," I told her. "And anyway, I like walking in snow."

"Wow," she replied. "You definitely are a crazy loon."

I wandered over to the bed and sat down, picking up my phone from the bedside cabinet. Call it an obsession if you like, but I spent countless hours every day inspecting the nearly always blank screen and checking the text messages. I had to laugh at myself, really, because even though it was a couple of months since I'd heard from Blake, I still held out a tiny shred of hope that he might get in touch. Call me stupid, but there was a possibility of, say, one in ten million?

The wonderful hot summer that we'd spent together seemed never to have happened, and to say that my heart ached at the thought of never seeing him again was definitely not an exaggeration. But then Michael's situation suddenly hit me, and I wondered what on earth I was moping about. After all, my gripe was just about a holiday romance, but Michael.... Well, he might have to go through life without seeing his daughter, and that was a very different thing altogether.

"Ruby? Earth to Ruby, are you listening to me?"

"Huh?"

"I've been shouting at you for ages." Rose had joined me where I sat on the bed. Clad only in her pajamas, she looked like a little girl, and even more so when she turned to gaze at me with those light blue eyes, identical to mine, and said, "Ruby, I'm going to resign from the job in the library." Straight and to the point—yes, that was Rose.

"Rose, for God's sake." I felt a twinge of annoyance at the whole library job scenario, and if she really was going to resign, then what had been the point of all the upset over it? On the brighter side, though, I knew the girls in Student Reception would be relieved that she was going. I didn't think Rose would ever win a popularity contest if they were on the judging panel.

"I know, I know. Please, Ruby, don't get mad. It's just that I don't think I'm cut out for it." And then, very shamefaced, she said, "I don't think I'm even suited to working in a school, and I never felt right about taking the job from you."

"What are you going to do then?" I asked irritably.

She went back to bed and brought her laptop to life

with a twitch of the mouse. "I'm thinking of law — maybe a solicitor's office. Mum said she'll have a word at her place. Apparently, there's an opening for a personal assistant to one of the conveyancing officers. I've been looking at their website. Look."

I nodded and looked at the screen with her. "Great idea. You can put your typing skills to good use, and legal work will be really interesting." Hopefully, that would be the end of the conversation.

Quickly I started to get dressed, pulling on a pair of waterproof walking trousers, a T-shirt, a warm fleece, and thick socks. Rose, watching me, said carefully, "You will apply for the library job when I leave, won't you, Ruby?"

I shrugged and sighed. "I'm not sure now that I want the job," I said as I filled my rucksack with a bottle of water, purse, phone, and snacks. "I might travel again."

"Hmm," said Rose. "What, go back to St. Malo chasing after that musician guy?"

I'd told her all about Blake on our recent night out when too many glasses of wine and umpteen shots had made my mouth run away with me. "Rose!" I said indignantly. "I'm not chasing after anybody."

"I don't know why you don't go out with James," she said. "Vanessa's seeing Craig, and…well, I'm going out with Steve tonight. All six of us could go out together, but as couples."

I didn't reply but shrugged into my waterproof jacket and pulled a hat onto my head. Glancing from the window, I remarked, "Oh look, it's stopped snowing." The sun, a weak glow in the cloudless blue sky, was already melting the thin covering of snow on the paths and the grass.

She came to stand beside me again and, encircling my waist with her arm, pulled me close, and said imploringly, "Don't ignore me, Ruby. James really likes you."

I hugged her back and then gave a small smile as I pulled away and wound a scarf around my neck, and zipped up my jacket. "So you keep saying, Rose. But you know, we don't choose who we fall in love with, do we?"

"Oh, go for your walk," she said with a sulky pout.

With my hand on the door knob, I turned back to her. "If I'm not home before you go out tonight, have a good time with Steve."

Her lips turned up in an unwilling smile, betraying the fact that she wasn't really mad at me at all...well, not anymore!

Chapter Ten

An icy wind cut right through me as I stepped out the back door. It penetrated even the thick layers I wore, sending a cold shiver down my spine. The orange glow of the sun, promising so much heat as I gazed at it from the bedroom window, was in reality as cold and unfriendly as a block of ice. I hunched my shoulders to my ears, slipping and sliding on the snow-speckled garden path as I made my way onto the High Street. Geese honked and spat viciously while ducks quacked and flat-footed swans ambled the cobbles as I walked down to the harbor, where tiny matchstick boats bobbed up and down on the white-tipped pointy waves.

I saw very few people as I marched quickly around the harbor wall, swinging my arms energetically and gazing out towards the deeper sea, where buoys, bright orange dots in the winter murk, danced gaily. Dogs barked and strained on their leads as their owners hurried along, eager to get home and sit by the fire or make a detour to the Bluebell or the Coal Exchange for a warming rum or whiskey or a thick, smooth sherry. I noticed that some of the shops already had Christmas trees glowing in the windows, and lights that flashed and threw lozenges of color—red, blue, yellow, and green—onto the paths, and that many of the pubs had festive menus prominently displayed.

My thoughts turned to Blake, and I wondered what he was doing right at that moment. Did he ever think of me? Did he wonder what I thought of him not contacting me? What sort of a person was he to just dump somebody as he had dumped me? Coward, that's what I thought—a coward not to ring me or even text. Okay, it's not ideal to be chucked by text, but it was better than nothing. Better than silence.

As was always the case, though, when I thought of Blake, my feelings veered from sorrow to hot burning anger all in the space of a few seconds. The urge to look into his grass-green eyes or smell the sweet scent of his skin was overwhelming. I'd like to watch him as he vaped, as his lips enfolded the machine, giving me hope that soon those very same lips would be placed on mine.

Get a grip, Ruby, I thought and, desperate to stop the thoughts from milling around in my head, I made a plan to walk to Warblington Cemetery and St. Thomas a Becket Church, and then along the shore to the Old Mill and the Royal Oak. I began to walk faster to keep warm. It was mid-afternoon yet dusky, and snowflakes began to fall swirling white against the dim sky, stinging my face like pellets from a gun. The cemetery was virtually empty but for a couple of hunched figures, creepy in the gloom, who were placing a great sheaf of pungent gold and crimson chrysanthemums against a small heart-shaped headstone.

I wandered past the church that squatted low like a dark beast surrounded by gigantic trees, their gnarled trunks too wide to span, and old crumbling headstones, the writing barely legible now and the bones beneath long gone to ashes. Deep notes from an organ and high-pitched singing resonated into the air. The heart-shaped stone laden with flowers was for a child, a four year old child. I traced the wording with my fingers. *With cherished memories...our daughter...Becky....*

Children, especially little girls, turned my thoughts to Michael and his despair on the day we went to the house in Bosham when he'd staggered into the garden like a hobo, his feet bare. He had a daughter, Leah, only two years old. A daughter he'd barely had contact with in that time through no fault of his own, but because of his girlfriend, Priscilla Fenton.

"Priscilla," I remembered thinking as I looked again at the black and white photo of her and Leah that hung on the wall. "It suits her." My hunch had been right. The child was Michael's daughter and, therefore, Mum's granddaughter. What was she to us? To Dad, to me and Rose? Step-granddad? Half-aunts? Yes, that must be right. Wow!

Priscilla, though, was an unusual name and, thinking about it, the only Priscilla I had ever heard of was the one that married Elvis, and she was dark and pretty too. Oh yes, and of course there was Priscilla, Queen of the Desert — but that's another story.

"So what happened?" asked Dad. "After she gave birth to Leah?"

"She dumped me," he told us as we all sat around him on the threadbare settee and chairs in his bare sitting room.

He wore slippers now, old and scuffed, and was hunched into a jacket that he'd put on over his threadbare jumper. The house was cold. "She told me I wasn't needed now. I'd done my bit."

I remember how we all stared at him in disbelief.

"Don't you see," he said, angry now, not with us but with the whole situation. "She wanted a baby, and she used me to get what she wanted. She sized me up, you know— good job, smartly dressed, expensive car, plenty of money— he'll do. She chose me and pretended to love me to get what she wanted…a child."

"Oh, Michael." Mum reached out tentatively and patted his shoulder.

He sat back in the chair, breathing heavily after his outburst. "We even discussed names and chose both a boy's and a girl's. We didn't want to know what it was, you see." He gazed at us and smiled sadly. "We had Luke for a boy." Shyly he turned to Mum and said, "Leah's middle name is May—I insisted on that."

"You need a good solicitor, Michael," said Dad kindly. "And I think we," he glanced at Mum, "Can help you with that."

My thoughts were so intense I didn't notice the tall figure standing at my side until he said, "Wow, Ruby, I don't know where you were, but you definitely weren't here in Warblington Cemetery. I said hello at least three times."

"Oh, God, sorry, James. I was miles away." I looked up into his open, smiling face and felt a sudden surge of—I don't know, was it happiness? Contentment? He wore a waterproof coat similar to mine, the hood pulled firmly over his head and even his chin, just his dark eyes staring out at me, shiny as sloes, and the tip of his nose red from the cold. He was holding a large bunch of — yes, you've guessed it, chrysanthemums. They shone out in the gloom as red as blood, smelling of the earth.

"I'm visiting my dad," he said, indicating the flowers. "Do you want to come?"

I knew that James had lost his dad when he was young.

"Yeah," he said, kneeling down at the graveside and busily discarding all the dead crumbly flowers to make room for the new ones. "He died when I was twelve. I don't know if you remember that." Slowly he shook his head. "A tragedy, a car accident. I really miss him. Well, we all do." Meaning, no doubt, his mum and his younger sister, Lara.

I nodded sympathetically and murmured that yes, I did remember him going home early from school one day, led from the classroom by a teacher, all the kids staring at James's baffled face.

"That's why I work in Sonic Engineering, you know." I glanced at him, frowning. "Because Dad worked there. I feel as if I'm sort of — I don't know, carrying on a tradition. Two of my uncles are there, and a cousin, Penny — she works in the offices." He laughed softly. "It's sort of a family thing."

He carefully wrapped the dead flowers in the old crinkly wrapping paper, ready for the bin, and then stood up, dusting off his trousers with gloved hands. The snow had stopped again, and the air smelled fresh and clean. Misty tendrils wound their ghostly way in and around the headstones like wraiths. I thought of James's dad, Mark, gone from him for such a long time and felt a sudden surge of compassion as I gazed at James's open, smiling face.

"Come for a drink with me, Ruby? The Royal Oak always has a fire at this time of year. It'll be warm and cozy." He turned and gazed along the shore, where we could see the stony beach and the sea, a light grey, lapping at piles of greasy-looking seaweed. "And it's not that long a walk."

"Yeah, I'd planned on walking to the pub." My phone beeped, and for a split second full of a stupid, irrational hope, I glanced carefully at the screen. It was from Mum.

Ruby r u okay? Snowing here! Be careful!

I replied straight away. *Bumped into James. Going to Royal Oak for a drink. Be home soon. Btw not snowing here! x*

Just as James had said, The Royal Oak was warm and cozy, the fire roaring like a lion in the massive fireplace. We sat on wooden stools, gazing into its orange center, mesmerized by the tongues of flames dancing up the chimney as, slowly, we sipped our drinks. I gazed around the bar, at the white-painted misshapen walls decorated sparsely with pictures of fishermen battling enormous fish and ships riding high on raging seas. Woven mats were laid haphazardly on the rough stone flags, and a group of people wearing green wellies and padded jackets stood idly at the bar, drinking and chatting, their dogs laid out long and hairy, snoozing, at their feet.

The smell of roasting meat and vegetables filled the air, and a waitress clad in tight black leggings and a white shirt and long apron hurried past, carrying large oval plates into the dining area. A Christmas tree, tapering to a majestic point and topped with a silver angel, sparkled in a corner, and tiny pink lights twinkled around the bar. Outside, the snow was falling again, the flakes small and fine against the backdrop of a darkening afternoon.

I told James about Michael and the little girl called Leah that he barely saw because of the influence of his evil girlfriend, Priscilla. I painted her so black that I wouldn't be surprised if James had a picture in his mind of Maleficent, Mistress of Evil. She had the same long dark hair, piercing features, and a cold black heart.

"He had a good job as a reporter for a local paper in Swansea but, because of the stress of it all after Leah was born, he had to give it up. He said he couldn't concentrate on his work any longer and found even turning up on time in the mornings difficult. Apparently, Priscilla was supposed to leave her rented accommodation and move in with him after the baby came, but she broke it off with him instead and said she would never allow him to see Leah."

James shook his head sadly and said, a frown etching his brow, "God, that's terrible! How did he buy the house in Bosham with no job?"

"He sold the house in Swansea that was left to him by his adopted mum and dad. Of course, the money he got for that wasn't enough to buy outright. Houses in Swansea are much cheaper than in Bosham, so he has a mortgage." James nodded as I carried on with the tale. "He bought the house in Bosham because he'd found out by then that his real mum lived in Emsworth, and he thought that being near his new family could probably be a good thing."

"Yes, I can see that," said James. "He would have needed the support after Priscilla dumped him like that."

"Yes, but the house purchase was held up, and he had to live at the pub initially. In the meantime, Priscilla contacted him and said she wanted to try again, so, desperate to see his little girl, he got the house ready for her and Leah. But she did the dirty on him, let herself into the house and cleared most of the furniture out, all new that he'd just bought, and took all the money from his bank accounts. Oh, and maxed his credit card to the limit."

"Wow! Not a nice woman! So he gave her free rein of his debit and credit cards?"

I shrugged. "He must have. A bit of a stupid thing to do, eh?"

"Especially as he knew what she was like, you know, dumping him the way she did and not letting him see his daughter. Has she met somebody else, do you think?"

"Michael thinks she has but doesn't know for sure. But yeah, you're right, not a nice woman."

"What's going to happen now?"

"Well, Mum and Dad have made him an appointment to see a solicitor friend of theirs. Actually, it's Mum's boss, Ralph Butcher. You know the solicitors Butcher & Steele?" James nodded as I carried on. "Michael has rights, so he must be able to have visits with Leah."

"Didn't he realize before that he had rights? After all, she is his daughter."

"I don't know, James. I think he thought he didn't have any because they're not married. He's a bit naïve, don't you think?"

James shook his head, in total bewilderment it seemed, and said, as he drained his glass and stood up, "God Ruby, after all that, I think we need another drink, don't you?"

I nodded and watched him as he went to the bar and

ordered more drinks.

"These should help," he said, smiling as he placed two small glasses of rum on the table. He'd also gotten a couple of bowls of crisps and peanuts for us to snack on and the menu, just in case. James picked at the crisps as we talked of other things.

I told him that Rose was going to give notice at the library, and he encouraged me to apply for it. I didn't say anything about my need to travel again and my compulsion to go to St. Malo in search of a musician called Blake Edwards, who hadn't even the common decency to break off a relationship with me as he should have. We had been talking of Michael being naïve, but I had the strange feeling the same thing could be applied to me.

There was a flurry of activity, and I noticed that the people standing at the bar were preparing to leave — finishing their drinks, buttoning their jackets, and putting on hats and gloves. The dogs hauled themselves up with a sigh. Music was playing quietly in the background. Lovely heart-wrenching music.

"Look," I said wryly. "Just because Rose said she's going to give notice doesn't mean she will. I don't need to tell you that I know Rose as well as I know myself."

"So," he teased, "If you said you were going to do something, would you definitely do it?"

"Yes," I replied, nodding my head and helping myself to a handful of peanuts. "I'm too boring and straightforward to do anything else."

"Ruby," he said, taking hold of my hand and softly kissing the palm. "You could never be boring."

I blame the effect of the rum because my eyes filled with tears, and I let James pull me close and kiss my cheek. His lips felt warm and dry against my skin. The door suddenly banged open, making me jump, and a group of people dressed as if for the North Pole surged in, followed by a burst of icy cold air and a flurry of snowflakes. Chairs noisily scraping the floor, they sat at a table and began to study the menu.

"What do you think?" asked James, fluttering the menu at me. "Shall we order, madam?" I started a bit at the "madam"—it reminded me so much of La Bar and the young waiter fluttering around me on the day that Blake had turned up to perform. Memories that I really didn't need at the moment.

Much later, fueled by food and alcohol, we crunched home through the snow, the air cold and crisp and the sky arching above us clear and black, set with tiny pinpricks of stars. I felt invigorated as we walked, my senses heightened to everything around me—the shushing of the sea and the cawing of the gulls, the strong smell of salt and seaweed, James's hand firmly in mine, and our icy cold breath puffing from our mouths like speech bubbles as we talked.

He took me right to the door, where he pulled me close and, gazing into my eyes, leaned forward and kissed the very tip of my nose. "I love you, Ruby. Always have, always will."

"James, I—"

"Ssh, it's okay." Gently he pushed my fringe from my eyes with his fingertips and, leaning forward again, softly touched his lips to mine. He smelled so good, spicy and aromatic. We stood together, our foreheads touching, his strong arms encircling my waist and pulling me ever closer and closer. My heart beat so hard I thought it would burst.

"I'll text you, Ruby."

He began to walk away but stopped and turned around, studying me intently, his head to one side, before saying, "Just wanted one last look."

A wonderful shiver ran up my spine, and I grinned at him, lips turned up in a smile before he walked away.

Chapter Eleven

It was the last day of term at school, and Christmas was rapidly approaching. The choir was in the hall practicing for their carol concert, and their voices, such beautiful young voices, were moving me to tears. We had a massive Christmas tree in the reception area, a silver one bedecked with streams of red tinsel and flashing golden lights, a beautiful angel crowning the top. Many of the students had been standing, staring at it as if in awe. As if they couldn't quite believe their school had such a fantastic Christmas tree.

"Wow, miss, the tree is awesome!" And I had to agree with them, it was.

"All thanks to the hard work of the Maintenance Team!" I kept telling them.

Just as she said she would, Rose had given notice at her job and already had an interview lined up at Butcher & Steele for the Legal PA position that Mum told her about. In the meantime, the library job was being advertised again with a closing date early in the New Year, so I had plenty of time to think about whether or not to apply.

I was still not sure. Something inside me wanted to travel again. I had a strong urge to go back to St. Malo, to stay again at La Petite Amelia and stand at the window gazing at the beautiful garden, with the sun on my face and the salty smell of the lapping sea hanging in the air. I had an irresistible urge to spend the evening in La Bar, sipping red wine in a dark corner while the crowds went crazy as the singer, a good-looking man with long dark hair cradling a guitar, took to the stage and serenaded me with "Ruby Tuesday."

Everything awaiting me in the future was still a mystery despite the things the tarot reader had told me. Still nothing from Blake, but I had to admit that I didn't check my phone with as much intensity as I used to. I was not so obsessed with the little beep that indicated there was a text message ready and waiting for me in my inbox. I still cared. I still wanted to know why he didn't get in touch, but since I had started seeing James, it didn't seem to matter as much as it had. There was something about James—I was not sure what. His kindness? His concern for me? His funniness and silliness? The way he looked at me as if he was going to love me forever and ever? I could go on and on, but as I said, there was something about James, something…oh, I don't know. I don't want to say it because it's such a cliché, but…. Well, he touched my heart.

I knew that Mum and Dad were secretly over the moon that James and I had become a couple. There was nothing they'd like more than to see me happy and settled with somebody who lived close by and to finally get that upsetting holiday romance out of my system. Oh, don't get me wrong, it couldn't be just anybody local—they loved James. They always had, right from when he was a little boy at school. He was always the good little boy, the one that obeyed his mum and dad without a second thought, and, as he got older, he was the calm steadying influence on his two close friends, Steve and Craig.

The three of them were always together. Rose and I would see them all the time sitting on the harbor walls fishing, their own makeshift rods and lines dangling in the water, or foraging for cockles in the sticky, slimy mud at Langstone, or riding their battered old bikes to Hayling Island along windy country lanes. They were fascinated by our identical looks and argued all the time about who was who until one day, as if a light bulb had gone off in his head, James said, "Ruby's the one with the mole!" Bingo!

Maybe it was because he had to go through his dad's death at such a young age, or maybe it was because he was just James. Whatever. He was a nice guy, and I felt lucky to have him. But why, then, did I feel so restless sometimes, as if there was a great big world out there and I was missing out on it? Rose was always lecturing me as if she were someone older and wiser, someone, with years of experience. "A classic case of assuming the grass is greener on the other side, Ruby. And it isn't, it really isn't—it's a mirage!" How Rose knew that I have no idea.

She was over the moon, too, because her dream of the six of us going out as couples had come true. Vanessa had hooked up with Craig and Rose with Steve, so James and I made a nice tidy six. Rose's dream had been realized and, do you know what? I thought she was secretly planning our wedding day, maybe all six of us together. I'd spied her looking in the window of the wedding dress shop, Dream Day Bridal, on the High Street so many times that she must be up to something. The dresses, while being identified as a bride's dream, with so many flounces and lace and long flowing veils, could also turn out to be a bride's nightmare! Or was that just me?

"Hey, Ruby, can I have a word?"

I looked up to see Katie, the library manager, standing next to me. "Hi Katie, how can I help?"

I liked Katie. She was a nice woman, maybe in her thirties, married, I thought, with a couple of little kids, even though she looked like a kid herself with her long multi-colored hair and Doc Martens boots. When I'd first started at the school, I was amazed at how many of the staff dressed so bohemian, slightly on the hippy side. Unfortunately, my thoughts then turned to Blake, who also gave off that sort of vibe.

"I just wanted a quick word with you," she whispered. "Look, Ruby, I'll come straight to the point. Are you going to apply for the library job this time?"

I grinned to myself as I wondered what she'd say if I told her I'd wanted to apply for it last time but had been warned off by my own sister. Instead, I just said, "I'm not sure yet."

"Oh." She looked disappointed. "Rose has done a good job, but…." She took a cursory glance over her shoulder. "I think you could really be cut out for it. You're so bookish and get on really well with the students. Why didn't you go for it before?"

"Well, I went travelling, and actually, I might be off again. So who knows? There's other interest in the job, though, isn't there?"

The break time bell shrilled, making us both flinch, giggling, hands to our hearts, and then there was pandemonium as students rushed out of classrooms and made their way, shouting and laughing, either outside into the cold frosty air or to the canteen for much needed refreshments.

"I'm not sure, but there wasn't a lot of interest when Rose got the job."

A group of people came wandering uncertainly into the reception area and came to stand at the desk, looking at me expectantly, and then the phone started to ring. Summing up the situation, Katie said, "I'll let you get on. Maybe we could have a chat when we're back at work after Christmas?"

I nodded as we wished each other a Happy Christmas and then turned my attention to the school's visitors, who had come for a meeting with a teacher about "our" Robert. The rest of the day passed quickly, and before I knew it, I was on my usual walk home with the two-week Christmas break stretching in front of me. I felt unusually lighthearted. Groups of students ambled along, talking about their holiday plans and seeming in no rush to get home, and I urged them to hurry and get back before dark. My thoughts turned to James, and I wondered what he was doing that evening. I hoped that perhaps we could go out, just the two of us, for something to eat and maybe a drink.

I walked quickly, my boots like slippers on my feet and my coat zipped up to the neck, together with a hat and gloves keeping me warm and cozy. With lamps shining in the windows and Christmas lights twinkling, home looked welcoming as I walked up the garden path. Although I was glowing from my walk, I was still glad to step into the cozy kitchen where Mum, Dad, and Michael sat companionably around the table, clutching mugs of tea and coffee. The oven was on, bathing the room in warmth and, from the smell, could only assume that some sort of fish pie was browning nicely in there. There was no sign of Rose.

"Hey Ruby," Michael stood up and enveloped me in a bear hug. Gazing at him, I saw that he looked tons better than he had when we'd seen each other in the house in Bosham. He'd transformed himself from the old down and out with the bushy beard and tatty clothing back to the smart, clean-shaven boy next door, and my God was I glad to see it. I took off my coat and hung it neatly on the back of the chair.

"Hey, Michael." We high-fived and grinned, whilst Mum told me to sit down as she pushed a mug of coffee over the table towards me. I helped myself to milk, definitely no sugar, and took a great gulp, licking my lips with pleasure as the caffeine shot through my veins.

"How's school today, number one twin?" asked Dad jokingly.

"Good, busy as usual. More so because of it being the last day of term. Where's number two twin?"

"Pampering herself upstairs," replied Mum, nodding her head towards the ceiling. "Getting ready for tonight."

"Oh, where's she going?"

"Aren't you all going out? Some sort of a Christmas do at the Coal Exchange?"

"Yeah, and I'm working," put in Michael. Michael had been helping Robert at the pub while hoping to get a job at the local newspaper, *The Emsworth Echo*. According to another contact of Mum and Dad's, they would be looking for a new reporter within the next couple of months. "So I can keep an eye on both of you and make sure you don't drink too much." He gave a short laugh. "I wouldn't want you to have a hangover tomorrow!"

"Yeah, good luck with that," I said, taking another sip of coffee. "I feel like a few glasses of wine tonight, although I did actually think that the 'do' was tomorrow night."

My phone beeped with a message from James. *Hey Ruby, I'll be round at 8 … can't wait to see you Jx*

Hmm, bang goes my cozy twosome with James tonight, I thought.

"It's gonna be a good night. Robert's booked a live band — they're supposed to be really good."

"Who are they?" I asked, thinking for one crazy moment that Blake might have set up a new band and was laying low in Emsworth until he could surprise me tonight with an extra special rendition of "Ruby Tuesday."

"They're a duo called Two's Company, a couple of women that do Motown, disco — you know, that sort of thing. The place will be rocking."

"Sounds good. I love that sort of music."

"Yeah, Robert's been a bit worried that the Bluebell was doing better on the live music front, so he decided to book this band even though they're really expensive. He's hoping the punters will stream in tonight."

"Oh, I'm sure they will," I assured him. "Everybody

loves a good live band."

"I have contacts, you see, from my old job in Swansea. That's what I specialized in, you know — interviewing new up and coming bands."

"I envy you that," I said, thoughts of Blake once again coming into my mind. Mum gave me a penetrating glance as I said, "A very interesting job."

A blast of steam hissed into the kitchen as Mum got up and peered in the oven at the fish pie. "This is ready. Anybody want any?" She set the steaming dish on the table and started to share it out onto plates while shouting loudly for Rose to come down and eat. "No, Stan," she said to Dad as, hopefully, he proffered a plate towards her. "We're going to that new pizza place tonight with Lenny and Sue, so you'd better not have any of this."

"Don't be mean, May," said Dad, disappointment evident in his voice. "I'm peckish. Just a tiny bit?" he cajoled.

Michael and I exchanged amused glances as Mum dumped one tiny spoonful on his plate before putting yet more on mine and Michael's and Rose's.

Rose came down and took her place at the table next to me. She nodded around the table, and I noticed that she still wore her pajamas but had styled her hair in a different way, and her face sparkled and glittered with make-up.

"You look like a fairy princess," commented Dad, as he nibbled at his meager helping of fish pie.

"Thank you," she said graciously, picking up a fork and poking about at her food. "How's it going with the solicitor, Michael?" she asked.

"Really good," he replied, picking up his mug and

drinking, and then, nodding at Mum and Dad for confirmation, said, "There's no reason why I can't have visiting time with Leah. It will probably be every other weekend, and maybe once during the week. Oh, and once she starts nursery and school, there'll be some of the school holidays too." He beamed around the table.

"Brilliant!" we said in unison.

"The trouble is, though," his face was downcast now, "Nobody knows where Priscilla is at the moment, and all this will have to go to court, so it could be ages before anything happens."

"It could happen sooner than you think," said Dad kindly. "The solicitor may already have an idea of where she is."

"Oh, and — " Michael almost choked on a forkful of the pie and, sitting back in his chair, breathing heavily and batting his hand in front of his face, said, "Too hot! Oh my God!"

"Ha," said Dad. "Serves you right for taking too big a bite! You should have had a small portion — like me!" He glanced at Mum, who poked out her tongue like a child.

"The house in Bosham is up for sale, so hopefully, I'll recoup some of the money that Priscilla took."

"You may get it all back when they track her down," put in Mum.

Michael frowned and said morosely, "Hmm, it could be a long job. Maybe it would be quicker to get a private detective onto her."

"Yeah," said Dad, slowly shaking his head. "But that will cost money, Michael."

"I know, but it's something to think about. I get mad

when I think what she's gotten away with." Scraping his plate clean, he checked his watch and said that he'd better go. Robert would need help in setting the pub up. He stood up, thanking Mum for the meal, shaking hands with Dad, and kissing us goodbye.

"The trouble is," he said sadly, turning around, his hand on the door handle, "The more waves I make, the more she'll try to stop me from seeing Leah. I know what she's like."

"It's got to be done," Mum said. "Be strong, Michael."

When he'd gone, Rose said, "I bet she's gone back to Swansea. Are they looking for her there?"

"I think so," replied Dad, looking hopefully at our plates like a starving man. "I'm meeting with Ralph Butcher tomorrow after morning surgery. Maybe he'll have news."

Looking at her phone, Rose suddenly squealed and nudged me so hard I almost fell off my chair. "Good God, Ruby, it's almost seven o'clock, and Steve's coming for me at half-past. I need to get dressed."

"James is coming at eight," I replied. "But I'll be right up to get ready."

"Go on," said Mum as I looked worriedly at the dirty dishes on the table. "Go get ready. Me and your dad can clear up."

"No," I could hear Dad say as I sped up the stairs to get in the bathroom before Rose took over. "I haven't the energy. I'm too hungry."

"Oh, for God's sake, Stan," said Mum irritably.

I giggled as, hastily, I locked the door and, flinging off my clothes, quickly got in the shower.

Chapter Twelve

James arrived well before our meeting time of eight o'clock. I could hear the murmur of his voice as he talked to Dad downstairs. Dad was starving hungry by now and wanting to talk about food, and was telling him about the pizza he would be enjoying soon, the largest they had in the Pizza Parlor in Havant, with several different toppings and extra cheese and extra olives, all washed down with a good bottle of red. He sounded like a condemned man ordering his last meal. I've got to say I felt nauseous even thinking about it.

Poking my head around the sitting-room door, I dragged James out before Dad could regale him with any more "food" stories. Holding firmly to his arm, we ambled slowly down the garden path, my heels clacking like castanets, and onto the High Street beautifully lit up for Christmas, with multi-colored lights looped between the lamp posts interspersed with smiling snowmen, Father Christmas's, and trumpeting angels. It was a clear starry night, the sky black and shiny, the air frosty and white. I shivered and pressed myself closer to James's warm body.

"Wow, you're looking good tonight, Ruby." He held me at arm's length so he could get a better look.

Secretly I'd hoped he'd say that. I'd dressed carefully in a short black dress, the bottom and neckline decorated with silver sparkles. I wore long silver earrings that glimmered when I moved and tights decorated with tiny colored jewels that shimmered as I walked. My make-up and hair followed the same sparkly theme, and I wore a silver shawl around my shoulders and carried a silver clutch.

"You're stunning," he told me as he pulled me close and nuzzled into my neck. "Umm, you smell good too."

"It's called Babe, your favorite." I was buoyed up and happy, looking forward to a glass of wine and to seeing Rose and Steve, Craig and Vanessa. I felt better than I had for ages. Totally revitalized, I intended to put Blake Edwards behind me and forget all about him. I was with James now, and that's where I intended to stay.

The pub was packed with warm, heaving bodies. Robert had been right. Live music was certainly bringing in the punters. Groups of people stood at the bar waiting to be served, and Robert, Michael, and a young girl I hadn't seen before, with short bleached hair and a nose ring, were rushing around pouring the drinks. Rose appeared from the crowds and beckoned to us with an outstretched arm, wearing a dress very similar to mine. I did a double-take. How did she know? They already had our drinks on the table as we gratefully sat down, and, reaching for my wine, I took a deep swallow of the ruby red liquid.

Vanessa, wearing her usual tiny mini-skirt and clingy top, long blonde hair falling around her shoulders in waves, clutched a massive glass full of a pale blue liquid teeming with cherries and slices of lemon on cocktail sticks and a little wooden umbrella. "Ta da," she said, holding her glass high. "Viva Espana!"

The band that Michael had raved about, Two's Company, appeared with a fanfare and launched into a cover of the Supremes "Floy Joy." The crowd went wild and started singing along and waving their phones in the air, clicking pictures from every angle. The two women had enormous curly afros threaded with tinsel and wore tight white cat suits that clung to every curve, showing acres of dark flesh. They had deep husky voices, and their dancing was smooth and fluid.

Annoyingly, I noticed that the television behind the stage had been left on. Nobody seemed to be watching it because they were concentrating on the act, so really, what was the point? I know I'm in the minority here, but I can't understand why people want to watch the telly when they're on a night out, especially on a Christmas do! Oh well, the subtitles were on and no sound. I suppose Robert must have forgotten to turn it off earlier.

After a foot-stomping encore, the two ladies went off to have a well-earned break. I saw them go outside, sashaying in their high heels, fur coats draped over their shoulders, clutching drinks and cigarettes. Somebody turned the telly up, and a band started playing.

"Wow," squealed Vanessa, looking in awe at the television screen. "It's that really cool new band, The Pilgrims.

You must check them out." She pulled Craig to his feet and started whooping it up on the dance floor, followed by Rose and Steve, and James, looking at me questioningly, held out his hand.

Shaking his head, he rolled his eyes at Vanessa's excitement, whispering that she'd had too much to drink, and then smooching closely, we both stared curiously at the screen where a band fronted by a cool looking dude strumming a guitar was playing catchy rock music. Gyrating sexily, the lead singer wore tight black trousers and a waistcoat, but no shirt, showing off his lean, tanned arms and chest, and a trilby that he wore tilted rakishly on his long dark hair. I noticed that his beard had been replaced by sexy designer stubble.

Vanessa squealed again, "Oh my God, the lead singer is gorgeous. Blake something. Check...him...out...!" She made a thumbs-up sign and carried on cavorting around the dance floor, Craig hot on her heels, followed closely by Rose and Steve.

Mesmerized, I gazed at the screen as the cool dude spoke, subtitles flashing. "Hey, yeah, I've been playing pubs and clubs in France, mainly St. Malo, desperate for my music to hit the big time. And now...well, man, this is a dream come true! I jammed with friends, and The Pilgrims were formed. We'll be touring the UK over the next few months. Dates to be released very soon. It'll be great to see all our loyal fans getting down and rocking at our concerts. Peace and thanks, dudes!" He made the two-fingered peace sign and gave a brilliant white smile, his glassy green eyes flashing, attractive lines crinkling at the corners of his eyes. I was rooted to the spot, the pub and the crowds ebbing and flowing around me as if I were in the middle of the sea. I could feel James's hand, steadying and warm, against the small of my back.

And then the announcer, his voice full of excitement, said, "Wow, check that out! That was Blake Edwards, the enigmatic lead singer with up and coming new band The Pilgrims. They'll be touring in the New Year, but in the meantime, check this out too…their debut single, 'Baby, You're a Doll'!"

My face frozen into place, I laughed and smiled, expecting at any moment for it to crack like a thin sheet of ice. Blurry and unsteady, a glass firmly in my hand, I watched the band as they performed on a massive stage lit with roving colored lights, watching Blake as he cavorted and preened as if he were born to it. His voice was amazing, even more strong and rocky than ever and, if I hadn't been so upset at his total betrayal, I could have been really proud. "Yeah, baby, you're a doll!"

It was okay, though, because nobody noticed the turmoil I was going through. Not even Rose, who, even though she knew about Blake and my broken heart, obviously hadn't put two and two together—hadn't thought for one minute that the "enigmatic" front man of this brilliant new band was her sister's lost love. And thank God, even James didn't seem to have a clue. "Lost in France?" Bonny Tyler, you don't know what you're talking about!

~*~

I'm dancing on a stage wearing red hot pants with bib and braces and high-heeled leather boots. The lights are so hot they're making me sweat so that my make-up, thick and dark, smears all over my face and my neck. There's a band playing, and the lead singer wears leather low-rise trousers, and his chest is bare. He strums a guitar and circles his groin seductively at the hectic crowd. His neck is corded as he screams into the microphone. The music is loud, so loud that it reverberates through the soles of my boots, tingles all the way up my legs, and flutters into my stomach and my chest.

He comes closer, and we dance together, shaking our bodies and swirling our heads around and around until our hair weaves together as one long glistening dark plait. "Hey, Ruby Tuesday," he suddenly says, "Listen to my song. 'Goodbye Ruby Tuesday, who could hang a name on you, when you change with every new day, still gonna miss you.'"

"For God's sake Ruby, will you shut up? You're mumbling and wriggling about — are you dreaming or what?" A hand roughly shaking my shoulder woke me up, and, opening my eyes with difficulty, one eyelash at a time, I saw Rose's angry face glaring down at me. "Shut up, or get up. Please!" she said nastily as she thumped back to bed, pulling the duvet over her head in disgust.

I lay there for a few minutes, recalling the dream. I remembered the manic dancing and the weird costume and the lights, sweat pouring down my face and stinging into my eyes. And then the dream faded and the night before came crashing into my mind. Blake and his band on the big screen, their growing popularity, talks of touring and excited screaming fans. He was on his way up, and I was just a woman he once knew. A woman he had a fling with for one holiday only. One hot summer holiday in St. Malo.

My anger grew, and my heart beat fast as I lay there thinking about the words of love he'd whispered in my ear —

that he would be in contact, that he would come to Emsworth to be with me, and that he cared. Lies, all lies! The urge to confront him was so great I wanted to get out of bed and travel all the way to France — right now! Why hadn't he contacted me? I really felt I couldn't live the rest of my life without knowing that crucial piece of information. The feeling was so strong I imagined sitting on the trundling bus as it heaved its way into Portsmouth, following the slow-moving crowds onto the bobbing ferry, where, in the same little café for breakfast, I would gaze from the window at the shiny, glassy sea as it rocked and rolled its way to St. Malo.

The bathroom mirror showed a tired troubled face, my skin still covered in make-up and glitter, sad remnants of the night before. Wearily I wiped it away with cotton wool and cleanser and crept back to the bedroom to find some clothes, careful not to wake Rose, the angry sleeping beauty.

I thought of James and his cold peck on the cheek as we'd parted the night before. I'd thought he had no idea about Blake, but did he? Had he hidden his feelings last night when The Pilgrims had been on the screen in all their glory? With a sudden panicked jolt, I tried to remember if we'd made plans to meet, but nothing came to mind. I would have to text later.

In the meantime, I had to clear my head, so, whatever the weather, I needed to be outside walking. Wrapping myself warmly in coat, gloves, and hat, I made my way downstairs. The kitchen smelled of frying bacon, and Dad, still wearing his dressing gown, was busy at the cooker. Mum, sitting at the table talking on her mobile — I assumed to Michael, as she mentioned court dates and visiting rights — gave me a little wave of her fingers as I let myself out the back door.

The cold hit me straightaway, making me gasp, a needling cold that pierced my thick layers like little darts. I almost envied Rose, snug as a bug curled into her warm duvet. The whole world was white and frosty, and I breathed out in soft plumes as I walked carefully down the slippery garden path and made my way to the harbor.

Frost rimed boats bobbed on the sea that, white and frozen as a painting, barely moved in the chilly breeze. Mist hovered above the water like a ghost. I walked briskly, breathing deeply, hoping to clear my hungover brain from thoughts of James and Blake, but however hard I tried, they just wouldn't go away. There was hardly anyone up and about at this hour, just a couple of dog walkers, their pets bounding along, tongues lolling, seemingly oblivious to the frigid air, so it was a shock when a figure suddenly loomed out of the murk. A very tall figure, so tall I had to crane my neck to look into his face. James.

My heart was beating so hard, and so fast I thought I might faint, yet with no hesitation, I gazed straight into his eyes.

"Well, well, Ruby Tuesday. Why aren't I surprised to see you here this early in the morning?" he asked with a grin.

Although his grin comforted me, being called Ruby Tuesday by James was a bit of a shock, yet I simply replied, "I couldn't sleep."

"No, neither could I."

"Look, James. I met Blake long before you and I started seeing each other, and...." I knew I was gabbling, but I couldn't stop.

He hunched his shoulders to his ears and said,

shivering, "Why don't we grab a coffee somewhere warm? It's too cold out here to talk. That little place on the High Street, Café Mocha, is good."

The place was almost empty, just a couple of people sipping drinks and a man tucking into a full breakfast, but toasty warm, the large windows foggy with condensation. The smell of roasting coffee beans filled the air. James brought the steaming drinks to the table, plus a plate of assorted flaky croissants and Danish pastries. We sat in silence for a few moments, stirring our drinks and looking at the food, although, on my part anyway, without hunger at the moment. The young girl behind the counter yawned, her mouth wide and cavernous.

"I'm glad I saw you," I told him brightly. "I was going to text later."

He nodded as he took a big slug of coffee. "Yeah, I suppose we need to sort this out."

"Yeah. James, I met Blake when I was in France, in St. Malo." I spoke very quietly, almost whispering.

He nodded, watching my face, staring at it intently. "I guessed that you had. There was something about the way you watched that band, so intense."

"I met him on the ferry. An up-and-coming musician, very sure of himself, very cool." James nodded again. "We arrived in St. Malo, and he disappeared, said it was good to meet me, and then gone in a puff of smoke." I took a swig of hot chocolate and carried on. "After about a week, I went to a local place called La Bar—a really good place…you'd love it—and bumped into him there. He was the regular act. We saw each other for the next three or four weeks of my stay—

you know, before Rose got in touch about Michael turning up. He assured me that he would be in touch and that we would see each other again, and that…. Well….” I glanced at him apologetically. “That he cared about me and would come to Emsworth.”

James drank his coffee, eyes downcast now.

The café door opened with a ching, and a couple walked in, stamping their feet and rubbing their hands together, faces red from the cold. They ordered breakfasts and drinks and rounds of toast in loud voices, shattering the quiet.

“Well, he kept in touch for the first couple of weeks I was back, then nothing—zilch. I texted him and rang, but nothing, no response whatsoever. And then last night I saw him on the big screen with his band. It was a shock, James.”

“Yeah, I should imagine it was.” He smiled a bit. “I could tell by your face that something was wrong, but obviously, I wasn’t sure what. Wow, I can’t believe he did that to you. What a jerk!”

“Yes. I have to admit I was surprised. I thought we had something, you know?”

James covered my hand with his, and it felt warm and steadying. “You have to sort this out, Ruby, one way or the other. We can’t carry on seeing each other if you still have feelings for this guy.” His dark eyes seemed to burn hot and shiny as he gazed at me.

“Are you dumping me, James?” I asked carefully, teasingly, hoping that my shaky voice wouldn’t betray me and that I wouldn’t burst into tears. Taking in James’s open, trusting face, I began to seriously question if I was doing the right thing.

"I have no choice, Ruby," he said sadly. "I love you —
always have, always will, ever since we were kids. But I can't
play second fiddle to anyone, let alone a hot shot famous
musician. I can't compete with that." He shook his head
vehemently.

"What do you want me to do, James?" I asked
desperately. The couple were talking to the man who'd eaten
the big breakfast about the weather and the tides, their voices
still loud and overbearing, so I had to strain nearer to hear
him.

He sat forward in his chair, elbows on the table, hands
clasped. "I can't help you there, Ruby. You have to work that
out for yourself — only you know how you feel. And well, the
thing that worries me the most is, if this Blake guy had kept
in touch and had come here to see you, you wouldn't have
started going out with me, would you?"

I didn't know what to say, so I sat there, dumb, tears
threatening to spill at any minute, but then blurted out,
"James, if I hadn't seen him last night on the telly, I could
have let it go. But…. Well, now I have to find out."

James nodded and said carefully, touching my hand
briefly with the tips of his fingers, "Yes, you need to set your
mind at rest."

I nodded, and my heart pounded as James drained his
mug, stood up, and, after zipping his coat to the neck, gave
me one final glance and said softly, "Take care, Ruby."

Before I could find my voice to call him back, he was
gone, the café door banging closed in the draught, leaving
only a blast of cold air swirling around inside.

Chapter Thirteen

Christmas passed in a blur with no James, and a heavy aching heart that, however positive I tried to be, wouldn't go away. I carried it around as if I was wearing a hair shirt. He came by while I was out walking, with a beautifully wrapped present and a card full of loving words, which I can only assume he bought before our break-up. Rose said he looked drawn and upset but was still adamant that I sort things out with Blake before we see each other again. I knew he was right to instigate this separation, but I was hurt, and I missed him, even though I thought of Blake too, and knew that the time to confront him was getting nearer and nearer. The New Year was looming, and a visit to St. Malo, where I was pretty sure I would find him, was definitely on the cards.

In total contrast to how I was feeling, my brand new stepbrother, Michael, was on a high. The solicitor had tracked down Priscilla, who was found holed up in a crummy flat in Swansea with Leah and a new guy, somebody called Ray

Lewis. The case was going to court the first week in January, with the assurance that visiting rights were a definite and that soon he could expect to be seeing his little girl on a regular basis. He went at his job behind the bar at the Coal Exchange with renewed vigor, the smile on his face as wide as the expanse of sea between Portsmouth and St. Malo, and, my God, that is wide!

To Rose's great excitement, she got the job at Butcher & Steele, so she wouldn't be returning to school in January. The decision to apply for the library job or not was pressing, and for the life of me, I couldn't think what I wanted to do. I didn't remember ever being in such a turmoil about so many things. So one day, over the Christmas break, I tracked down Mum, who was lounging in the sitting room watching *It's a Wonderful Life*, and plonked myself down next to her on the settee for a talk. Luckily Mum had the whole Christmas break off from work too.

We were alone in the house, Rose having gone out with Steve — they were definitely becoming a serious item — and Dad, to Mum's great pleasure, was paying a visit to the Coal Exchange to have a beer or two with Michael, at Michael's invitation. From what Michael had said to me and Rose, I thought he was trying to pay Dad back for sorting out his bill at the pub after Priscilla had bled him dry.

The room was cozy with the glow from the wood-burning fire and the twinkle of the Christmas tree lights. The smell of burning wood and oranges hung in the air. "Now then," Mum said, looking full at me. "I suppose it's been a strange Christmas for you without James?"

"Yes," I said sadly, nodding my head. "But I had to tell

him about Blake, especially after we saw him on the telly with his band."

"Yes, of course, you did. Blake's done well, hasn't he? A famous musician — wow! And from the pictures I've seen, he's a very attractive young man." Glancing at the television screen, I saw James Stewart rushing around in a demented frenzy, eyes almost bursting from his head. "I do love this film," Mum told me.

"I do too. Yes, if I wasn't so mad with Blake, I'd be really proud. And yeah, you're right, he's very handsome."

Mum smiled as James Stewart gave Donna Reed a big hug and kiss and, as the whole cast smiled at the camera, the closing credits scrolled slowly down the screen. She turned to me, giving me her full attention. "It's got to be said, though — James is very attractive too." I nodded in agreement, and then she said, "What do you want from this, Ruby? How do you feel about these two? Have you discussed it with Rose?"

"Well," I said, thinking hard, concern furrowing my brow. "I'm extremely...extremely fond of James. In fact, I can't really imagine my life without him." Then I shook my head. "No, I haven't said anything to Rose. She's really caught up with Steve now, and we don't seem to spend as much time together as we used to."

I glanced at Mum, who said, "Rose has got her own life now too, I suppose, and she seems fond of Steve." She smiled at me. "Yes, James is a very nice boy. Your Dad and I are upset at your splitting up, but obviously, we can see the reasons. What about your feelings for Blake?"

"I'm angry with Blake for not getting in touch — for hurting me so bad — yet I'm glad for him that he's made the big time." I paused for a minute and then said, "I told James that if I hadn't seen Blake on the telly, I could have let it go. I was enjoying being with James, but it brought it all back and…. Well, I know what I'm going to have to do, Mum."

"Yes," she said. "Confront Blake—go to St Malo? But what about holiday from school? When would you be able to go?"

"Look." I showed her the screen of my phone where a new website, "Tickets are Good," was selling The Pilgrim's concert tickets. "They're touring the UK in March and April, so I thought, okay, I'll go see them in concert, maybe in Portsmouth. Hopefully, I'll be able to go backstage, but it's not guaranteed I'll be able to. He might say no, or say he doesn't know me, or never heard of me! After all, if he really did want to see me, he'd have gotten in touch, wouldn't he?"

"Yes, I see what you mean."

"But look." I showed her some earlier dates that were featured on the website. "They're doing an 'Up Close and Personal' mini-concert at La Bar in St. Malo in February, for Valentine's, I think, which coincides with the February half-term. And no need for backstage passes or anything like that, because the concert is happening in the bar—voila!"

"I don't know why you wanted to talk to me, Ruby. You've got it all worked out anyway."

"I need to know if you think I'm doing the right thing, Mum. Going all that way, spending all that money, to confront Blake. And I can't go, like, now anyway, which puts my relationship with James at risk. And not knowing whether to apply for the library job…I need your advice."

"Okay, this is what I suggest. First thing, yes, go and

confront Blake. At least you'll know the score. Second, *James* has refused to see *you* until you've sorted things with Blake, not the other way around. And thirdly, go for the library job. It's what you always wanted to do. And as for when you go to France, February half-term is the first opportunity you'll have!"

"Okay, but what if there is a genuine reason that Blake hasn't been in touch? I forgive him and move to France. What about the library job then?"

"Yes, that could happen, but if you move to France to be with Blake, you'll have made your decision, and you won't see James again. And as for the library job, so be it—there are other jobs here or in France."

"Oh, God! Dilemma, dilemma!" I wailed, falling back into the soft cushions of the settee, my head in my hands.

"All that aside, just apply for the job, Ruby," urged Mum. "Apply for it. You might not get it, and even if you do, there's a strong possibility you wouldn't even start until after the February half-term because of DBS checks and references, so you'll have confronted Blake by then."

"Yes," I agreed. "As long as the 'Up Close and Personal' concert isn't cancelled, I'll definitely catch up with him then, and he'd better watch out!"

"Good," said Mum, raising an arm high above her head and shaking a fist. "Fighting talk…Warrior Woman!"

Giggling, we cracked open a bottle and toasted my decisions, or should I say Mum's, with a flourish.

Taking a sip from her glass, Mum said, "Oh, by the way, Ruby, changing the subject, I know, but…." She lowered her voice to a whisper. "Michael met up with Nick, his Dad."

"Wow, that's great. Does Dad know?"

"Oh yes," Mum assured me. "I haven't mentioned it to Rose yet, though."

"When did they meet?"

"Last week in Horndean. Michael went to his house, met Julie, his wife — not the daughters yet, I don't think. They seemed to get on okay."

I frowned and said, "Why didn't you tell us about it before?"

"Michael wanted to see how it went first. And he was keen to tell his dad about the impending court case and that soon he might be able to see his granddaughter."

I nodded and then said carefully, aware that I was treading on thin ice, "What about Nan and Grandad — do they know about Michael yet?"

Mum shook her head. "No. I'm not sure what to do about that, Ruby."

"I suppose you'll have to tell them, won't you?

Mum, her eyes downcast, carefully studied her nails. "Why should I tell them?" she said sadly. "They made me give him away — they don't deserve him."

"Mum!"

"No, Ruby, please." Glancing at me, tears hovering in her eyes, she said, "Just go and fill in that application form. That's what you should do next."

I knew I shouldn't pursue the subject any further, so I backed off. Hugging her, I said, "Thanks, Mum," and went from the room, rushing upstairs to my laptop.

~*~

I didn't have to sneak out of the house this time

because everybody knew when I was going, why I was going, and what I was going for. Rose told me to go for it, but I was aware that she was worried I might track down Blake and finish with James for good. Although, really, James had finished with me just before Christmas on that cold frosty day when we'd had coffee together in Café Mocha. He'd texted on Christmas Day and a couple of times after that, and I'd told him I was going to St. Malo, but so much time had gone by with nothing resolved that I'd be very surprised if he'd be waiting for me when I got back. Nobody had said anything, but I thought maybe there was a new girl on the scene and that James had found the courage to move on.

It was a dank, dismal day, the sky arching above, grey as iron, speckled with mournful cawing gulls. Gazing from the window of the bus as it trundled along, I glimpse Langstone, the tide a long way out and the sea just a thin line, the stony beach deserted. Even on the bus, the smell of mud was very strong. But then, thank God, it disappeared as we neared Cosham and then finally trundled into the city of Portsmouth. I shuffled in dense chattering crowds, my rucksack on my back, onto the swaying ferry, and then stood at the rail, clinging on with gloved hands, a stiff sea breeze slapping at my face until it shone bright red.

I couldn't believe it had been more than six months since I'd last been on the ferry. That I'd travelled alone all the way to St. Malo with hope in my heart of a great adventure. So now, a seasoned traveller, I felt confident enough in the future to go further afield on my own. Well, it was very unlikely I would meet another Blake to entertain me on this particular journey, so as it was so cold on the deck, I wandered inside to the same little café to warm up. With a surge of excitement, I thought of the booking I'd made at La Petite Amelia for a whole week and how glad I would be to see Amelia and Georges again.

Drinking creamy hot chocolate and gazing out the window at the glassy green sea rolling and heaving, the day of the library job interview came to mind. I was thrilled to finally get the job. Talking about my starting date with Katie, going over my duties and responsibilities, and just sitting in the library with the students and chatting about books and reading made me realize just how much I'd given up for Rose, and I was over the moon that she'd finally found a job that suited her and that I'd finally found mine. I was looking forward to starting the job properly when I returned to school after the break.

Now all I had to do was sort things with Blake, and everything would be plain sailing — pun intended, seeing as I was on a ferry rolling its way across the sea to France! What a year last year had been — all the dilemmas we'd been through as a family, and the most important thing, of course, Michael seeking us out. Really, he'd turned Mum's life around, and now that she was able to see her granddaughter, Leah, that was just the icing on the cake.

My thoughts turned to the day of the court case but were quickly gone when suddenly there was pandemonium as people began to stand up, gulp down their drinks and swallow last morsels of food while collecting belongings and making their way out onto the cold deck. I realized with a jolt that we were arriving in St. Malo. The journey had flown by, so I quickly put my rucksack on my back and began to follow the slow-moving crowds.

The grey sea tipped with white rose and fell, sharp pointy little waves peaking and troughing, peaking and troughing. A great flock of pesky seagulls squawked and dived as I made my way down the creaking gangplank, shuffling along as if I was shackled with a chain gang until once again I was standing on French soil. I smiled to myself, looking forward to another adventure and The Pilgrim's concert at La Bar. All I could say really was, "Look out, Blake Edwards, here I come!"

Chapter Fourteen

La Petite Amelia was exactly the same, and Amelia and Georges just as warm and welcoming as they had been back in the summer. They showed me to my room, the same one as before, where I wandered around, unpacking my clothes, bouncing eagerly on the bed like the little girl I'd once been — to test the mattress — and gazing from the window at the garden, still beautiful in the thin February sunshine. The lawn glowed thick and green, and lustrous color still shone from the borders.

Sitting on a comfortable chair at the window, I texted Rose and Mum, and then, with only a slight hesitation, texted James to let him know I'd finally arrived in St. Malo and that I hoped he was well. A sheaf of leaflets and cards on the bedside table caught my eye, and, thumbing through them, I came across a flyer for La Bar, advertising their up and coming events.

The Pilgrims were heavily billed in great bold letters

and showed the one date in February for their "Up Close and Personal" mini-concert. There was a picture of the band, all young men with long flowing hair, Blake posing in the middle wearing tight trousers, a bare chest, and a sultry expression. Frowning, I wondered what had happened to Blake's band T-shirts. He certainly didn't seem to wear them anymore.

Suddenly curious, I googled them, searching for their debut single, "Baby, You're a Doll." I'd heard it before but listened again to the heavy bass guitar and screaming vocals. "Oh yeah, baby, you're a doll, doll doll, you make me rock and roll, roll roll, you kill me when you move, move, move, and make me wanna groove, groove, groove." Hmm, okay, I wasn't a song writer, but compare those lyrics to, say, "Ruby Tuesday," and would "Baby, You're a Doll" make the charts, or did people nowadays not listen or even care about song words?

For a split second, I wondered what on earth I was doing in St. Malo, searching for somebody who, clearly, didn't want me and who, clearly, couldn't write decent song lyrics. I immediately felt bad. Blake was on his way up a long hard road, and I was comparing the words of his songs with classics written by the Rolling Stones. Was I losing it? He would obviously improve with time and experience.

My phone beeped, and a message from Rose appeared on the screen, wishing me good luck, and would I please let her know as soon as I found Blake. Mum replied in a similar vein but, as yet, there was no reply from James. My heart sank. It had been weeks since I'd seen him, and, not really wanting to admit it even to myself, I had to face up to the fact that I missed him. I missed so many things about him.

His warm hand holding mine, his tender kisses, our crazy conversations, and our long ambling walks when we talked and talked and talked.

All these thoughts swirled around and around in my head, but resolutely, I pushed them aside and, shrugging on a jacket, decided to go out. Maybe a brisk walk along a chilly beach would make me feel better and, once I'd got the impending meeting with Blake over and done with, surely that would cheer me up too. It was hanging over my head like an executioner's axe.

My phone beeped as I made my way out of the B&B and down to the tiny secluded beach, where I'd spent so many hours sunbathing in the summer. Glancing down, I saw that at last, it was a message from James.

Hi, yes, I'm okay. I hope you find what you're looking for, Ruby. Take care. Thinking of you. J x

I'd dreamt of doing this, of coming back to St. Malo, to walk the sandy beaches and sit in a dark corner in La Bar drinking red wine and watching Blake perform on the stage. But now that I was here and all my dreams coming true, I wasn't sure if I wanted to be here at all. What had Rose lectured me about? Something about the grass being greener on the other side? I vaguely remembered her words. "A classic case of assuming the grass is greener on the other side, Ruby. And it isn't, it really isn't, it's a mirage!" Well, I was beginning to think she could be right, but only time would tell—oh yes, only time would tell.

My thoughts went back to the day of the court case and what an eye-opener it had been. I recalled the dark old fashioned room and the scary-looking judge who had turned out to be so kind. I recalled the musty smell of the courtroom, the dark, somber brown of the seating and the paneling on the walls, and the judge, presiding like a god high up in his chair, wearing a long black gown and a light curly wig. His features were sharp as pencils, and his gaze from hooded eyes as penetrating as a mighty eagle's—or, I think with a shudder, a vulture's. I felt, in this dark, gloomy place, that I'd gone back in time by a hundred years or more and that at any moment, people would come streaming through the old oak door wearing shawls and clogs. It amazed me that this man had the power to say whether or not my stepbrother, Michael Fisher, would be granted access rights to his daughter, Leah.

Mum, Dad, and I sat quietly on a bench watching the proceedings. Rose couldn't get time off so soon in her new job, so it was just the three of us as support for Michael, who sat nearby wringing his hands with anxiety, his face white and pinched. Priscilla, her black fringe dangling in her eyes, lips a pale sheen of pink, sat almost proudly with her boyfriend, Ray Lister, a great hulk of a man, broad shoulders hunched beneath his coat. He had huge meaty hands but the face of a child, all snub nose and doleful blue eyes. Mum and I exchanged a glance, Mum's eyebrows raised as if to say, "Hmm, an interesting combination."

Michael's solicitor, Ralph Butcher, took to the floor and gave a heartfelt speech, outlining the facts of Leah's birth and the subsequent breaking up with Michael by Priscilla—Ms. Fenton—with the words, "You're not needed now. You've done your bit." And also the fact that she had said that she would always prevent him from seeing his daughter and that she had pretended to love him to get what she wanted—a child. It was pointed out that Mr. Fisher had been traumatized by the break-up so soon after his child's birth and had suffered a breakdown resulting in the loss of his job, a job with a local newspaper that had not only given him a very generous salary but that he had excelled at. He then talked of the house in Bosham that Mr. Fisher had bought for the sole reason that Ms. Fenton had agreed to live there with him, but immediately took back her word on this and proceeded to steal his money — in fact, to bleed him dry — and once again, left him, taking her daughter with her.

I watched Priscilla's face change at Ralph Butcher's words, all the various emotions flitting across her face, none of which were sadness or even shame. Her expression was more defensive and even gloating than anything else. She read as easily as a book. I noticed Ray Lister giving her sneaky sidelong glances, his smooth pudgy face bland. Oh, to know what he was thinking.

The solicitor went on to say that Mr. Fisher was now employed, had sold the house in Bosham, and was in the process of buying a property in Emsworth close to his recently reunited family, where he would be able to provide a warm and loving home for his daughter. He recommended visiting rights of every other weekend, Friday to Sunday, the starting date to be agreed between both parties, and once during the week, Wednesday afternoon, which would be reviewed when the child was of age to attend nursery and school. At the end of his speech, he gave a slight bow to the judge and quietly took his seat.

Priscilla's solicitor took his turn, outlining the facts that Ms. Fenton had told him. That she wasn't keen on Mr. Fisher having visiting rights, as she didn't want her daughter to be confused by the erratic presence of her father; that she didn't feel she could trust him to maintain any visiting rights; that she only wanted what was best for her child, blah blah blah. I felt sorry for the poor man for his attempt at having to bulk out his speech with absolutely zero concrete facts. There was nothing he could say against Michael, as all the faults lay at Priscilla's door, and all the real facts had already been said by Michael's solicitor, Ralph Butcher.

There was a brief, tense silence before the judge spoke, his voice surprisingly warm and reassuring, belying his forbidding looks, as he said, "After listening to both sides of this somewhat sad story, I find Mr. Michael Fisher to be a man with a good heart, who has been prevented for the past two years from forming a close and loving relationship with his daughter, Leah Fisher. I fully agree with Mr. Fisher's solicitor, Mr. Ralph Butcher, that Mr. Fisher be granted visiting rights with his daughter of every other weekend, Friday to Sunday and every Wednesday afternoon. This arrangement is to be reviewed when Leah Fisher becomes of age to attend nursery and school." At this point, he fixed his steely gaze on Priscilla and said, "You will be in contempt of court if you breach a court order."

I remember then the sighs of relief as the proceedings ended and the judge stood up and disappeared very suddenly through the black curtain behind him, putting me in mind of a coffin vanishing into the ether at a cremation. There was a scuffle of feet as we all trooped outside, and I saw Michael's joyous expression as he raised his arm in the air and shook his fist in celebration of such a brilliant outcome to the struggles of the past two years.

The beep of my phone brought me back to the present, and I saw I had a text from Rose, asking if I was okay and wishing me luck for tonight. Oh my God, yes, The Pilgrims concert was tonight and, glancing at my watch, I realized that I really should be getting ready. What should I wear, though?

Blackness stood hard at the window, and the garden, shrouded now in near darkness, looked creepy in the gloom, the branches of the trees appearing deformed and twisted. Primulas glowed pink as a child's night light, and a soft patter of rain began to fall. I pulled the heavy crimson curtains across the window, hiding the view, and went to take a shower.

Gazing into the mirror, I carefully applied make-up, blow-dried my hair, and after dressing in jeans and boots, I wound a scarf casually around my neck and slung a leather jacket over my shoulder. Yes, definitely a rock-chick look for The Pilgrims. You couldn't get more rock and roll than Blake Edwards. Taking a glance in the mirror, I gave myself a thumbs-up sign and, letting myself out of my room, went downstairs for a drink in the bar to get myself in the mood.

The bar was cozy with lamps dotted around, throwing pools of light onto the wooden floors, and a real fire crackled majestically in the massive stone fireplace, reminding me, with a stab of nostalgia, of that lovely snowy day in the Royal Oak with James. Couples sat at tables drinking wine or elaborate cocktails, and most of the stools at the bar were taken by a group of men who chatted animatedly in broken French while enjoying their pints of beer with gusto. I drank a glass of wine with Amelia and Georges, who, when I told them about the concert, said they were big fans of The Pilgrims and had seen

Mr. Blake performing many times at La Bar.

They obviously didn't connect the young man I'd spent so much time with in the summer as being Mr. Blake, as they didn't say anything about him or ask me who my companion had been. I suppose they thought it was none of their business who this crazy English girl wanted to go out with or why she was back here holidaying barely six months after her initial visit. Or perhaps, as was more than likely the case, they'd simply forgotten.

"You enjoy St. Malo?" asked Georges

"Oh yes," I told him eagerly. "It's a fantastic place."

"You come live, maybe?" asked Amelia.

"Oh, I don't know," I told them with a shrug. "I have family in England — Mum, Dad, and a twin sister."

"Oh my God," said Amelia, raising her hands to her face, her eyes large. "There is two of you?"

"Two of you?" echoed Georges.

"Yes," I said. "She's called Rose — my identical twin!"

"You bring her here. We would like to see this other one of you, Ruby."

"Yes," I said before saying goodbye and taking the walk to La Bar. "Maybe next time I will."

There were crowds milling around outside La Bar as I neared it, and two beefy-looking men were on the door checking tickets and bags. People chatted eagerly in French and in English and, as I walked inside, I noticed that there was a table displaying T-shirts and hoodies, the band name The Pilgrims etched on the front in thick letters, together with a picture of the four guys, a mass of long wavy hair, tight trousers, and bare chests, Blake always resplendent, in the middle as the lead singer, the draw of the group. As he certainly seemed to be with the number of girls I saw literally swooning over him with the words, "Mr. Blake gorgeous," and "Sexy Blake." There were also posters of all sizes, even life-size ones. If it had been Blake's dream to become a pin-up, it was certainly about to come true.

Putting the T-shirt into my bag, I queued at the bar, listening to the loud rock music that was playing—music by Bon Jovi, Aerosmith, Whitesnake, and Free, and then made my way through the crowds, managing to find a dark out of the way corner where I could merge into the shadows. But not before a red rose for Valentine's was pushed into my hand by one of the bar staff as he weaved his way amongst the crowds, carrying a large overflowing basket.

It was standing room only, as most of the tables and chairs had been cleared away to make room for a makeshift stage, where a drum set and microphones were already in place. As it was only a small place, the crowd was close and hot bodies jostled against each other, as if in a sauna or a steam room. A burst of excitement shot through my veins along with the red wine, as well as dread at what I would say to Blake when I finally got to confront him after the show.

Without warning, the music suddenly stopped, Jon Bon Jovi silenced in his prime, and the lights dimmed. The silence was long and intense, so intense that everybody seemed to be holding their breath until all of a sudden, a loud drum roll sounded and the lights on the stage glared bright white and hot. A loud, manic cheer came from the crowd, and everybody raised their arms and flashed their phones, and before I could blink, the opening bars to "Baby, You're a

Doll" reverberated everywhere, around the walls, the ceiling and the floor, buzzing through my body like a dentist's drill. And at last, they were there — The Pilgrims, live on stage. The already excited crowd erupted!

Chapter Fifteen

"Hey Blake, there's a bird out here, calls herself Ruby — wants to talk to you."

The young guy stood back, letting me go through to the small backstage area where the band was chilling out after the show. He chewed gum, popping it at regular intervals with his tongue, and arrogantly looking me up and down as if I was a prize heifer at a cattle market.

Blake appeared in the doorway, still wearing his stage clothes of the tight black trousers and unbuttoned waistcoat, bare hairy chest on display. He frowned, his head tilted to one side. "Ruby? Ruby Tuesday, right?" I nodded, and he said, "I'd sing the song, but — you know, the old pipes." He put a hand to his throat as though it hurt and then brought a cigarette to his lips held tightly between his fingertips, palm upwards, and took a deep drag.

"Wow, you look good. Come in, come in." He beckoned me with his head, and I followed him into a small, sparse room.

The other three members of the band were relaxing lazily, their heavily booted feet up on chairs, smoking cigarettes and weed from the pungent smell and chugging beer from cans cold and beaded with moisture. I'd waited, hanging around in the bar area, until the crowds of fans had left. Until the band had signed autographs and posed for pictures, all part of the "Up Close and Personal" concert. I'd been there for hours.

He looked smaller than I remembered, not much taller than me, and pale, washed-out somehow without his summer tan. There was no denying that he was handsome and sexy — yes, definitely sexy — and sinewy, muscular. A weird sort of predatory appeal like Iggy Pop. He pushed a can into my hands and, taking one for himself, pulled the ring out and took a swig, saying, "How ya doing then, Ruby?"

Disappointment flooded me, a feeling so acute I wanted to stamp my feet and burst into tears. *Is this what I've come all this way for?* I thought. *Is this it? Just a casual how ya doing Ruby?*

"Do you remember me, Blake?" I asked.

"Yeah, sure I do."

All thoughts of congratulating him on the band and his success went right out of my head, and without thinking, I whispered urgently, "You stopped getting in touch." I was aware that the other band members were watching us, sizing me up, and trying to listen to what we were saying, "Is there somewhere else we can talk?" I asked him, my eyes flicking to the three guys.

He pulled on a jacket and said, "Yeah, come outside then."

"You didn't get in touch," I said again as we stood

outside in the cold, shivering. "I was worried about you. I texted and rang, but nothing."

"Oh, yeah, I had my phone stolen." He took a deep glug from the can and then wiped his mouth with the back of his hand. His lips looked as red and ripe as strawberries, and from what I could remember, were just as tasty.

"You had your phone stolen?" I asked incredulously, "So, all those months when I was upset over you, you'd just had your phone stolen? You mean, if you hadn't had your phone stolen, you'd have kept in touch?" A chilly breeze circled around us, making me hunch my shoulders to my ears.

"Yeah. Well, probably, but I had no way of contacting you, Ruby. Hey, I'm sorry, babe. I didn't realize you were upset."

I had an awful burning pain in my heart, and it was clattering away in there like a living thing, making me breathless. "You didn't realize I'd be upset? But Blake, I thought we had something together. You said you'd come to Emsworth to see me—you promised." I hated whining, but I couldn't seem to stop myself.

"Yeah, well, I had no number for you, Ruby. Then the band took off…. Look, you know, back in the summer, we had a blast." He pulled a packet from his pocket and lit another cigarette, inhaling deeply.

"You used to vape," I said moodily, folding my arms over my chest against the chill.

"Yeah, well." He shrugged and took another drag, smoke spilling from his mouth in a long thin plume. "Pressure, you know. But I gotta give it up, no good for my voice." I nodded again, and he said, "Ruby, we had a—what do you call it? Holiday romance? A fling? Yeah, even you said it was a holiday romance. You liked a guy back home called James. Is that right?"

My heart sank as I remembered my teasing words, my attempt to be oh so world-wise like Blake, cool and sophisticated. I could kick myself.

The gum-chewing guy from earlier poked his head out into the cold and said urgently, "Hey, Blake, Viv's on her way."

"Okay, mate, thanks." Blake, looking at the ground, took one last drag of his cigarette before flicking it away into the darkness. It lay on the ground, a tiny smoldering orange light.

"Viv?" I asked, my heart pounding. Surely he could hear it.

Before he could reply, a tall blonde woman came outside to join us. She was as statuesque and beautiful as a plus-size model, making me feel tiny and gauche as a child. She wore tight skinny jeans with towering high heels and a low necked top from which her large breasts spilled like squishy pillows. She went to Blake and, putting a possessive hand on his arm, drawled, "Hey, honey. You okay? How'd it go?"

"Yeah, good," he replied, and when she glanced over at me, he said, "Hey Viv, this is Ruby. Ruby, Viv."

Viv looked at me questioningly as I stammered, "Um, yeah. I met Blake a while ago here in La Bar." I hated Blake for putting me through this, for not explaining who she was, for standing there, head bowed, and staring at the ground in embarrassment. I glanced at him, but he remained silent, unresponsive. Desperate to know, needing to know, I asked her, "Are you Blake's girlfriend?"

"Girlfriend?" she said, giggling a bit and shaking her head. "I'm his wife, sweetie." Blake, cringing, stood stock still, glad, I suppose, that it was her and not him who had told me the truth. "Almost our three-year anniversary already, isn't it, honey?" She put a casual arm around his shoulders and pulled him close. He was so ill at ease that I very nearly felt sorry for him.

So, the truth is out, I thought. *He was married all the time — even our holiday romance was a lie!*

Desperate to get away, I turned then and began to run, Blake's voice calling for me echoing in my head. "Ruby, come back."

And then Viv's voice. "Oh, for God's sake, Blake, leave her. After all, she's just another one of your groupies!"

I ran past the other band members and the gum-chewing guy, who gawped at me, wide-eyed, and then out of La Bar, slipping and stumbling in my high heeled boots over the cobbled paths, past all the little gift shops and bars, their doors firmly closed for the night. I ran along the sea wall, where I could hear the faint sucking of the choppy water as it crept like searching fingers along the sand.

I kept on running, my breath ragged and heavy, away from my memories of the summer before, away from Blake's glassy green eyes and strawberry-lipped kisses, away from his silly French accent and husky rendition of "Ruby Tuesday." I ran into La Petite Amelia, quiet now and dark, everybody in bed, the fire from earlier a tiny red smoulder and the smell of wood smoke in the air. I ran up the stairs to the sanctuary of my room, where I threw myself onto the bed, my head in my hands.

I cried then, for a long, long time, heart-wrenching sobs tearing at my body, hot salty tears running down my face and soaking into my jeans. I cried until, head pounding and worn out, I curled into a ball tight as a fetus and, pulling the duvet closely around me, fell into a deep, dreamless sleep.

~*~

Even the chattering of the gulls was soothing, reassuring as I stood yet again on the swaying ferry, holding onto the deck rail with cold fingers, watching the silver shores of St. Malo gradually recede into the distance. Would I ever return? Hmm, maybe not. There were too many sad memories of this place to ever make me happy again. I'd stayed in my room for most of the day after the showdown with Blake, only venturing out for a short walk along the beach, crunching on the stones, head bent and hands deep in my pockets. The weather had changed from frosty sunshine and blue skies to grey driving rain and raging wind, and on the second day, with a heavy heart, I packed my bag and, with an excuse to Amelia and Georges about a family crisis, left La Petite Amelia.

"Come back with the one who looks like you, Ruby," pleaded Amelia.

"Yes," echoed Georges. "Come back soon."

Thoughts of Blake occupied my mind constantly. I imagined him as he was last summer, the man of my dreams, my hero, with that charming boyish smile. And now he was a rock star, a hardened, cynical sex symbol, suddenly older, bordering on seedy, and an adulterer. Had it not been love but a girly crush? My heart pounded erratically, and the thought, *What on earth am I going to do now*? flitted through my mind. I missed the Blake I thought I'd known, the happy-go-lucky up-and-coming musician. The Blake that had never really existed, the Blake I'd conjured up in my head, the almost perfect young man, talented and honest, and not the cowardly and weak liar that he'd turned out to be.

I thought of Blake's wife, Viv, and her comment about me just being one of his groupies. Just another girl he'd used to cheat on her. I'd had a suspicion of another woman, but a wife? No way!

James, I thought suddenly. *James is the only thing in my life that could make me feel clean again.* But why would he want me now? No, I'd blotted my copy book with James, and there was definitely no going back.

I disembarked from the ferry at Portsmouth, once again shuffling along in the chattering crowds, not only my rucksack weighing me down, but grief too, and sadness for all the hopes and dreams that hadn't been realized in St. Malo. As the bus trundled its way to Emsworth, I gazed from the window, admiring the view of Langstone's stony beach and, again, not minding the stench of the mud as it wound its way like smoky tendrils through the window. People wearing wellies and carrying buckets gathered cockles from the wrinkled sand. I was content, in a way that even I couldn't understand, to be almost home.

I longed to see Mum and Dad and Rose and watch their concerned faces as I told them the tale of Blake Edwards and my broken heart. That thought spurring me on, I went at a trot down Emsworth High Street, which was busy as usual with people wandering in and out of the shops and pubs and cafes. The smell of hot pasties and baking bread streamed from the baker's, and a chilly wind blew in from the rough grey sea.

A dark blue car that I recognized as Nan and Grandad's was parked outside the house as I hurried up the garden path, and to say that my heart sank like a stone at the sight of it is no exaggeration. As I quietly let myself in through the back door, I heard raised voices from the sitting room.

I recognized Nan's wailing tone. "Oh, how could you? How could you keep this from us?"

And then Grandad. "Yes, you're out of order, May. This is a family thing. We should have been told."

"I didn't know what to do," said Mum, her voice panicky. "We gave him away. I didn't think you'd want to see him. I've been in turmoil about what to do."

There was an intense silence before Nan wailed again. "Oh, May, we did what we had to do at the time, but we had a right to know," and burst into noisy sobs.

And then Dad, his voice hopeful, said, "Um, anybody want coffee? Tea?" And when there was no reply, just more heartfelt sobbing, he said, "I'm going to put the kettle on anyway."

I dashed up the stairs out of the way just as the sitting-room door opened, and Dad blundered into the kitchen to make the tea. I heard the hiss of the kettle and the chink of mugs and spoons. Rose was in the bedroom, curled up on her bed reading when I crept in and, with a sigh, lowered my rucksack to the floor.

"Oh my God, Ruby!" She jumped up and enveloped me in a hug and then, pulling back slightly, looked me full in the face and said, "It's really good to see you, but you're back early." I nodded. "It didn't go well?" she asked. I shook my head as, slowly, she led me to the bed. "Sit down and tell me."

"He's married, Rose. He was cheating on his wife the whole time we saw each other last summer."

"Oh, Ruby. I could kill him for that. Well…." She spread out her hands, palms upwards. "Welcome back to the drama downstairs. Just what you need, eh?"

I grinned. "I know. I came straight up here, even sneaked past Dad in the kitchen. I so did not want to get involved."

"Yeah, as soon as I heard Nan and Grandad arrive, I made myself scarce. I had a feeling what it would be about. I don't know how they found out, though."

"Well, I can see Mum being upset, but the decision to put Michael up for adoption was made by all three of them — well, four really, including Mum's boyfriend, Nick. What do you think, Rose?"

"It's a tough one. But don't forget how young Mum was at the time and how she'd have been influenced by Nan and Grandad."

I nodded, realizing how true that was.

A car screeched to a halt outside, the thunk of heavy doors opening and closing and then footsteps on the path. Curious, I moved over to the window and, twitching the curtain, peered out. "Oh no, this is really bad timing."

"What?" Rose came to stand beside me and looked from the window too, her face close to mine, two identical faces side by side, which would, I thought, look pretty funny if anybody was watching.

"It's Michael, carrying a bundle that's wriggling about very much like a two year old child."

"Leah!" said Rose, her mouth gaping open in surprise.

I shook my head in both excitement and disbelief. A slice of pink face set with two glistening dark eyes peeked from Michael's arms and seemed to stare straight up at us, "Yes, it sure is. Now the proverbial will hit the fan!"

Chapter Sixteen

"Now then," I said, looking around me at the semi-circle of tiny upturned faces. "Today, we're going to be reading this book." I held it up and pointed at the cover. "Would anybody like to tell me what the book is called?" Several hands waved in the air, and I pointed one out, "Okay, Thomas."

"Um...*Mr. Stink*, Miss."

"Yes, that's right. This is a book called *Mr. Stink* by a writer called David Walliams, and this will be our book to read for the whole of this week. Okay?"

"Yes, Miss." The sea of tiny heads nodded, and one bright spark, Robbie Eastwood, a cheerful grin splitting his face, two fingers pinching his nose, said, "Pooh, Miss, I don't want to read about a man who stinks!"

There was a lot of high-pitched giggling. "Okay, calm down now. Come on, Emma, Rosie." And then, turning my attention to Robbie, I said, "I promise, Robbie, you won't be able to smell the man we're reading about. Now come on, heads down."

Gazing around at the small group of children eagerly reading the book to be discussed this week, some laboriously following the words with an outstretched finger, a dart of happiness shot through me at the fact that I was now the library assistant for the school. It was my job, nobody else's. Not Rose, not Angie in Attendance, or anybody else that had applied for the job, but mine! The tarot reader had been right on that score. I was aware of my manager, Katie, bustling around, tidying shelves, picking up books and putting them back in place, answering the phone when it rang shrilly from the front desk and talking to teachers as they popped in to make inquiries.

The book club had been assigned to me. I was in sole charge of picking one book a week to be read and discussed by a group of children from each school year, and so far, fingers crossed, it was proving really useful. The children seemed to be enjoying their reading more than ever, and they loved the debates we had when we'd finished each book when we discussed the book in-depth and decided whether or not it was an okay book, a well good book, or an awesome book!

As much as I was enjoying my job, though, I'd been pretty down since I'd gotten back from St. Malo and after I'd tracked down Blake. I kept going over everything that had happened. Seeing, again and again, Blake's wife, Viv, standing there, so beautiful, her long blonde hair cascading on her shoulders, her red lip-sticked mouth turned up in a sneer, laughing at me for being just another of Blake's conquests. Just another of the stupid girls he'd taken in and serenaded with his rock star looks, charm, and voice. I felt stupid and foolish so, even though nobody knew anything about it apart from Rose and Mum and Dad, I'd laid low for a while, only going out to go to work and for the occasional walk. I still hadn't gone on a night out with the gang, although there wasn't really a gang anymore, just a foursome of Rose and Steve and Craig and Vanessa.

Nobody mentioned James and the overwhelming feeling that he'd found somebody else raced around and around in my mind until it drove me crazy. I assumed he'd found a nice girl who wouldn't mess him around. He didn't want a flighty girl called Ruby Tuesday, who had suddenly left him in the lurch to go to St. Malo in pursuit of a rock star. Oh no, he wanted somebody better than that. Somebody more dependable, somebody he could count on. After all, who's to say she wouldn't do it again in the future? Who's to say she wouldn't go off in search of greener pastures if they ever married and had children?

For some strange reason, I hadn't dared to contact him. How could I? I knew he'd said that he understood my need to go to France to find out what my feelings were for Blake, that we couldn't see each other until I knew, but how could I now get in touch and say, "Oh hi, James. Things didn't work out with Blake, so can we carry on from where we left off, please?"

Every time I went for a walk, I hoped and prayed I would bump into him. I kept my eyes peeled in Warblington Cemetery, hoping he'd be kneeling at his dad's grave replacing the old crumbly flowers for new, or walking the seashore to the Royal Oak, where we'd had a drink together on that cold, snowy day that seemed such a long time ago now. But it didn't seem to matter where I went. He was never there. No James on Emsworth High Street going in and out of the shops or the pubs, or sitting on the harbor wall, legs swinging, enjoying the approaching spring sunshine. No James wandering the beach at Langstone or hunched over on the rippled sand digging for cockles and winkles. No James anywhere, and my heart ached to see him again.

Even texting seemed intrusive, and something that I just couldn't bring myself to do, although my eyes were constantly drawn to my phone, hoping a message from him would appear. It reminded me of waiting for contact from Blake, and because that had driven me totally mad, I didn't want to repeat that. Did I? The only thing I could do was speak to Rose, ask if she'd seen him and if he'd asked about me. On thinking about it, though, I was sure she would have told me if he had.

Although nowadays Rose was very elusive, preferring to spend her free time with Steve rather than me. A far cry from when I was away in France, and she cried on the phone because I wasn't there to spend the holidays with her. Don't get me wrong, I wasn't complaining. This was how it should be. Everybody should have their own space. Yeah, even twin sisters.

As luck would have it, thinking about Rose must have conjured her up from nowhere, as on my walk home from school that very afternoon, I bumped into her coming out from work at her new job at Butcher & Steele. It was a balmy day for the end of February, and the sun glowed very yellow from a blue sky, just a few black-edged clouds floating around threatening rain for later. Rose looked good wearing a black suit with a red blouse tucked into the skirt, and she'd tied up her hair showing little red earrings that dangled from her ears and sparkled prettily as she moved. She wore red lipstick too and looked smart and business-like, carrying a black briefcase, quite at odds with me and my walking boots and rucksack.

When I asked if she had time for a talk, she suggested we go to Café Mocha for a coffee and, albeit slightly hesitantly, as that was where I'd seen James for the last time before I went to St. Malo, I walked with her down the High Street and into the café, the door opening with a loud ching as it had before. There was an older lady on the counter this time, wearing a smart pink overall, who made friendly conversation with us as she took our order, oohing and aahing at the fact that we were twins and telling us that her grandmother had been a twin, and she'd always been fascinated by the subject. The aroma of strong hot coffee beans mixed with countless fried breakfasts and well-done toast hovered in the air.

The café was busy, with most of the tables full, but we managed to find one by the large window, still foggy with condensation, that looked out onto all the comings and goings on the High Street. People, as they always did, stared at us as we sat down and gave grins and slight nods of their heads, to which we nodded back.

Rose added milk and sugar to her coffee and took a sip, leaving a very faint lipstick mark on the mug, which straight away she wiped off with her thumb. "What's up, Ruby?" she asked. "Are you okay? You've seemed so down since you got back from France." She gabbled on. "Oh, don't worry, I can understand why. I could kill that Blake for what he's done to you!"

I smiled a bit and said, "Yeah, it was a disappointment, but…. Well, really, if I hadn't seen him on the telly that night at the Coal Exchange, I probably wouldn't have pursued it. But…." I drank deeply. "That's not to say it didn't bother me, though."

She nodded and took another sip of coffee and said, "It spoiled everything for you and James too."

"Well, that's what I was going to ask you about. Rose, have you seen James? Have you spoken to him? Does Steve know anything?"

She shrugged and said, "Why don't you ring him or text? Or call in to see him."

"I can't." I shook my head, my heart beating fast.

"Why not? He might be waiting for you. He'll want to know what decision you've made, won't he?"

"I'm not sure. He told me that he understood why I was going and that I needed to find out why Blake had stopped getting in touch, but he didn't tell me to contact him when I got back."

"Do you really need to be told everything, Ruby?" she said irritably. "If it was me, I'd have gone to see him by now — or texted, or done something!"

We grinned at each other, and I said, "We do everything so differently."

"Yeah — and we're twins!" said Rose.

"Hmm. Being twins doesn't mean we're the same person." There was a short silence before I told her quietly, "I'm afraid he's met somebody else." I brought my mug to my lips, both hands wrapped around it — for warmth, I suppose.

I felt cold and shaky inside.

The door chinged open, making us jump, and a young woman came in, awkwardly trying to maneuver a stroller through the door, followed by two very young gabbling children who ran about between the tables as if they'd been let out of jail that very day. Rose and I exchanged a glance, and I knew that the children had reminded her of our half-niece, Leah, just as they had me.

"Don't be daft, Ruby. James loves you. He's not going to find anybody else he cares that deeply about in the space of a couple of weeks, is he? Really, you don't seem to know much about relationships."

"Oh, and you do?" I shot back.

"Well, yes," she said coyly. She had to speak louder over the noise of the two children pounding about with their sturdy shoes on the wooden floor. "Steve and I have been talking about getting engaged." She looked down at the table and then flicked her eyes back to me. "But you've got to work on them, Ruby—men have to be worked on!"

"Wow, engagement. That's great, Rose!" I put my hand over hers where it lay on the table between us. "But working on someone? No, that's not my style. If somebody really wants you, they shouldn't have to be worked on!"

"Well, you need to do something, or you'll lose him." She stood up and, smoothing her skirt down and picking up her briefcase, said, "Look, sorry Ruby, but I've got to go. I'm going straight to Steve's for tea. I'll see you later tonight when I get home." She put some money on the table, saying the coffees were her treat.

I nodded when something that Rose had said finally

worked its way into my brain and, as she began to walk towards the door, I said, "Rose, how do you know that James loves me?"

She shook her head, wrinkling her nose as if she didn't understand what I was going on about, and said, "Of course he does. It's written all over his face. But surely you know that? Go get him, Ruby!"

~*~

With the lady on the counter's voice telling the two small children to "Settle down, please," echoing in my head, I left the café just after Rose had gone. In fact, I could just about see the tail end of her in her black suit, happily swinging her briefcase as she walked jauntily down the cobbled street towards the harbor and to Steve's house. James lived not too far away from Steve and, before I knew what I was doing, instead of turning back away from the High Street towards home, I was following Rose, deciding in that split second that I would go and see James, and put an end to this worry and indecision once and for all.

He lived with his mum and sister in a semi just off Slipper Road, a lovely house surrounded by a large mature garden planted with lots of leafy trees and flowery borders. His dad had held a managerial position in Sonic, where James worked, which must have accounted for the big beautiful house they lived in. Nervously I walked up the driveway, noticing that there was no car parked outside, so they might not be in, but the garage door was closed, so perhaps the car was in there, nicely shut up for the evening. It had been a long time now since James's dad had passed away, but it must have been tough for Jacky, his mum, especially having to care for two school-age children on her own when he'd died.

Taking a deep breath, I knocked timidly on the door, with no idea what to expect. I hadn't seen James's mum for ages. A pretty young girl with long wavy dark hair opened the door and peered out at me. She was dressed in a short denim skirt with thick black tights, and a T-shirt with a picture of Lady Gaga on the front, along with the words Born this Way. She looked so much like a female version of James that I did a double-take. This must be Lara, his sister.

"Hi, um, is James in?"

"Oh, hi. It's Ruby, isn't it? Or is it Rose?" She looked confused.

I smiled. "It's Ruby." I pointed to my nose. "I'm the one with the mole. I just want a quick word with him if that's okay?"

"He's not here," she told me. "He—"

A voice echoed from inside. "Who is it, Lara?"

"It's Ruby," she shouted back, and there was a bit of a kerfuffle as James's mum appeared in the doorway, a curious look on her face. She was a lot younger than my mum and looked pretty hip wearing black leggings and denim shorts. She, too, had long dark hair and very dark eyes, and pale milky skin. Freckles ran wildly across her nose.

"Well, hello there. Come in, come in, Ruby. It's so good to see you again."

"Hi. I hope you don't mind me calling in. I—"

"No, not at all, not at all."

I followed her through a cozy kitchen that I noticed had one of those really cool looking Aga cookers and into the sitting room, where she invited me to sit on a really comfortable looking squashy leather settee. Awkwardly I sat down, putting my rucksack at my feet. She sat opposite, perched on the edge of a leather chair, as Lara hovered in the doorway, asking if I wanted tea or coffee or a cold drink. Juice or milk?

"No, no, thank you, it's fine. I've just had a coffee with my sister in Café Mocha. I just wanted a word with James."

I glanced around the beautiful room, at its cream-colored walls hung with interesting black and white pictures, one of which was set in London and featured a bright red bus smack in the middle of all the dark color. Another was of my hero, the man with the mole, Roger Moore himself, holding a cigarette and drinking what I assumed was a martini, the glass slap bang in front of his face. Wow! James's Mum was really cool!

"Oh, I do like that place. We go there sometimes, don't we, Lara?" said James's mum, looking at her daughter where she still stood by the door. "And with your sister? You're like two peas in a pod, you two. I often see you out and about in Emsworth and was so pleased when James said he'd been seeing you."

There was a short silence before Lara, coming to sit beside me, said, "James isn't here."

"No," said his mum. "He's working away for a couple of weeks, although it might be extended, in Southampton — at the other branch of Sonic. He's doing really well there. But of course, you must know that, Ruby."

"No, I don't actually," I told her. And I don't know why — maybe it was his mum, Jacky's, friendliness and kind worried expression, or just the build-up of so much tension after the drama with Blake and the upset of still not seeing James — but I put my head in my hands and, not for the first time recently, burst into a bout of noisy sobbing.

Chapter Seventeen

Michael was visiting again with Leah — it was his mid-week visiting night. I could hear her excited giggling and talking as I was getting changed in my bedroom. Rose wasn't back from Steve's yet, so there'd be just me, Mum, Dad, Michael, and Leah for tea, and, from the aroma weaving its way around the kitchen, chicken casserole was on the menu again. My mind wandered fleetingly to the first time Michael had turned up with her, the day when Nan and Grandad were already here, and Nan was having a meltdown about not being told about Michael having found Mum. It was the first weekend of access for him, and, as he said later, to find Nan and Grandad here as well was what you might call a bit of a shock.

I remember mine and Rose's first glimpse, that tiny slice of face set with glistening brown eyes peeking from Michael's arms, and then her staring up at us at the bedroom window, followed by her startled expression when we both appeared in the sitting room doorway. "Two same ladies," she said, pointing a chubby finger. "Two same ladies at the window." She stole several sneaky glances from beneath her eyelashes as we kissed Nan and Grandad hello and sat down on the settee. Nan was quiet now, just a half-hearted sniff as her red-rimmed eyes eagerly followed Leah all around the room.

Leah wore cute denim dungarees over a yellow shirt with tiny brown suede boots, and her dark hair was tied up in a high ponytail with a bright yellow ribbon, gauzy tendrils touching her cheeks as if they were a frame and her face the picture. And oh, what a face! Just imagine a combination of Michael's boyish snub-nosed innocence and Priscilla's chiseled cheekbones and slant-eyed beauty, and that was Leah May to a tee.

She walked around looking at us one by one, confident for a two year old. Mum and Dad were sipping their tea, Nan and even Grandad sniffing and red-eyed, me and Rose watching her just as much as she watched us, sizing each other up, and then suddenly, pointing at Michael, she said, "This my Daddy. He nice."

"Yes," I replied and, pointing at Rose, said, "This is Rose, your, um...."

I thought for a minute or two until Rose put in, "Your half aunt. And," nodding towards me, said, "This is Ruby, your other half aunt."

Leah giggled, showing tiny white teeth and a sliver of a pink tongue. "Half-aunt Rose and Half-aunt Ruby. Funny." She giggled uproariously, throwing herself against Michael's legs, her face in her hands. "Two same ladies," she said again and giggled some more.

"Yes," explained Rose. "We're twins, Leah. That's why we're two same ladies."

"Twins," Leah repeated thoughtfully over and over again. "Twins."

Michael joined in and, squatting down beside her, pointed at Mum and Dad and said, "Your nan and grandad."

"Nan and Grandad," she repeated, gazing seriously at Mum and Dad, before moving on to mine and Rose's nan and grandad, Lily and George.

Dad, who had been very quiet until now, spoke up. "Your great-nan and great-grandad," he told her.

She considered them both for a minute or two, and then, hands on hips, her little head on one side, she looked intently at Lily and said, "Oh Great-Nan, why you cry? I make you better." And before anyone could even take a breath, she'd climbed up onto Lily's lap and hugged her hard, snuggling her head into her chest. Well, if there was ever a volcanic explosion of tears, this was it, even putting my recent bouts of crying in the shade. I didn't think there was anybody in the world, and especially Great-Nan Lily, who could resist such a sweet child as Leah.

We all talked then, around and around, Nan and Grandad explaining to Michael why they had encouraged his mum, May, to give him up for adoption when he was born.

"We didn't know what else to do, did we, George?" Nan said, looking tearfully at Grandad as she cuddled Leah harder and stroked her hair. "May was too young to marry her boyfriend, Nick. We thought you'd have a better chance in life with an established married couple who had a home of their own, who both had good jobs. That's why we thought the people in Swansea would be ideal for you."

"Thinking about it now," Grandad said gruffly as he sat leaning forward, his forearms on his thighs. "It was the wrong choice to make. Maybe we should have kept you and helped May to bring you up, but it didn't seem like a good thing to do at the time."

"Hindsight is a great thing," said Dad, slowly shaking his head, and then, turning to smile at Mum, who sat beside him, gently patted her hand.

"Exactly," replied Michael. "You did the right thing. I had a great childhood. My adopted mum and dad were good people. I just knew that one day I wanted to find my real mum." He looked gratefully at Mum, who smiled at him. "And I have, which I'm really happy about. And I've found a fantastic step-dad too, and two beautiful half-sisters."

Dad inclined his head graciously towards him while Rose and I simply crossed our eyes and poked out our tongues. He fixed Lily and George with a stare and nodded his head. "I wouldn't have you two either if things had gone differently, so — anything that happened in the past is in the past, well and truly."

Lily sat forward, leaning towards Michael when a grouchy little voice piped up. "Don't squish me, Great-Nan." Leah's face appeared from Lily's chest, flushed and red, her hair dishevelled.

"Oh, sorry, darling," said Lily, mortified as we all laughed.

Michael said, "Everything happens for a reason. I have regrets about what happened between me and Priscilla, but there'd be no Leah if I hadn't met her."

"And that," said Great-Nan Lily, bending at the waist carefully and kissing the top of Leah's head, "Would be a tragedy!"

A bossy little voice shouting up the stairs brought me out of my reverie. "Half-aunt Ruby, it tea-time. Nan says hurry up — or get cold."

Taking one final glance in the mirror, I ran downstairs immediately, a smile on my face. I didn't want to upset the guvnor! And by that, I didn't mean Mum!

~*~

Blake's music seemed to play all the time. Everywhere I went, I heard the hard-rocking rhythm of the drums, the beat of the guitar, and the wail of his voice. It was on the jukebox in the Coal Exchange, in the Blue Bell, and pumping out from the radio and the television. Their debut single "Baby, You're a Doll," peaked in the charts, so I was informed by a group of students at school who, being ardent Pilgrims fans, were very impressed and even awed when I told them I had met the lead singer before he hit the big time. "Wow, Miss, really?" and "Is he really that good looking, Miss?"

I was shocked to realize I had no idea about the charts anymore. At the tender age of twenty-two, they weren't something I was interested in following. As Blake and I had agreed, the old music was the best. Anyway, whatever, their second single, "You Do It for Me," was released hot on the heels of the first one, also racing up to the top of the charts in record time. And exactly what the "It" meant in the title of the song, I had no idea.

Secretly I watched their videos on my phone. Curled on

my bed, my eyes fixed on the screen, I watched Blake's every move, the rest of the band invisible, blotted out somehow by the charisma of the lead singer. But wasn't that how it should be? All the great lead singers seemed to have the talent for holding an audience in the palm of their hand. I watched him, lithe and sexy as a panther, sinuously cavorting with scantily clad dancers as vocal cords bulging like thick wires, he screamed into the microphone.

I was amazed in a way at the change in him, this heavy metal rocker, who in the not so distant past had serenaded me with a soft voice and a gentle strumming guitar as sweet and innocent as every school girl's dream. Maybe the fans of the old acoustic Blake would boycott him just as they had Dylan and Bolan, raising their arms in horror or sulking in a corner, saying, "He's gone electric!" in indignant voices.

I still hadn't seen or heard from James and doubted very much now that I would. His mum, Jacky, had told me he was working away and would be for the next two weeks or so, but also that he'd been offered a long-term contract at the Southampton branch of Sonic, so he'd been thinking of relocating there. So there was my answer as to why I hadn't seen him out and about around Emsworth for such a long time.

"It's a managerial position," she told me proudly. "And at his young age, it's an honor to be offered it, really. He's doing so well for himself."

After my sobbing outburst, she had made me strong hot coffee and put assorted biscuits on a plate, and we had settled down to talk. Lara too, who, unlike Jacky, knew all about my relationship with James—that I'd gone away to St.

Malo in search of my "rock star boyfriend" and that James had been heartbroken.

"Heartbroken?" I asked them happily. "Are you sure he was heartbroken?" I told them tiny snippets of what had happened and that I'd been badly let down. I also told them I missed James and wanted him back but that I was afraid to contact him in case he'd found the courage to move on with somebody else.

"I don't think he's met anybody else," Lara told me. "He likes you too much, Ruby."

"He's too busy working anyway," said Jacky. "He's very focused on saving. He wants to buy his own place, and while he likes going out with his friends and enjoying himself, he's always wanted to get married and have kids." She shrugged as if to say, "What am I supposed to do with him?" Maybe not realizing how lucky she was to have a son like that.

She chatted on. "He's always been a sensible boy, and even more so since his dad died. I suppose he felt when his dad had gone that he had to look after me and Lara." She gazed into the middle distance. "It was a lot of responsibility for a boy of only twelve years old."

I agreed with her and said that I remembered when it had happened and James going out of school on that awful day.

They both encouraged me, just as Rose had, to text him or ring or go out in active pursuit and track him down. I imagined myself running around the slippery cobbles of Emsworth, brandishing a massive net and capturing him as if he were a slippery fish or a fluttering butterfly. But, no, that definitely wasn't me. And so the time went by and still no word.

I spent a lot of time when I wasn't at the school going on my usual long walks, but I also had a brand new job of looking after Leah for an hour or two when Michael was working at the pub. Now that the weather was warmer, I was able to take her to the beach, where she paddled her tiny toes and foraged for shells, clutching a bucket and spade in her pudgy hands. I taught her how to make proper big sandcastles decorated with bubbly seaweed and surrounded by a moat. I showed her how to search for scuttling crabs in the clear rock pools and how to skim flat stones from the water's edge.

We dug for cockles and took them home to eat, even though she wrinkled her tiny nose at the fishy smell as they bubbled in the pan. Sometimes Mum came with us, or Dad, and occasionally Rose, but usually it was just the two of us, me and Leah. Partners in crime. And the strange thing was that Leah, without even knowing it, was helping me, soothing me, easing my heartache over Blake, and now James too. For all of us, it seemed that she'd come into our lives at exactly the right time.

~*~

My phone rang, buzzing away in my rucksack. I was tempted to leave it. I was very nearly home from work, just stepping onto the High Street, but decided I'd better not. It could be an emergency. So, fumbling in my bag, I put my phone to my ear and said, "Hello?"

"Hello, Ruby?

"Yes, this is Ruby."

"Ruby, Amelia here. I have Mr. Blake. Will you speak?"

Puzzled, I smiled and shook my head, thinking immediately it was Rose carrying out what you might call "a very bad taste prank!" It was April now, and the weather hotting up a little, the sun beating down in a bright yellow glare making me squint. Sweat ran in little rivers down my face and my neck.

"Hello, Ruby, Mr. Blake wants to speak, will you?"

"Who is this?"

"It is Amelia from La Petite Amelia. You know me, remember, Ruby?"

I heard a voice faintly in the background. "Tell her I only want a few minutes."

My heart pounding so hard it reverberated in my ears. I said, "Blake?"

There was a kerfuffle as if the phone had been taken away from someone, and then a voice, deep and clear over the line. "Hey Ruby, it's Blake." And then, with a laugh, "Do you remember me?"

"Of course I do," I replied, and then, "Is it really you?" I'd carried on walking and had reached the harbor and was sitting on a bench, looking at the view, my hair blowing around my face in a welcome salt-laden breeze. The tide was out, and the sand stretched ahead for miles, as rucked up and wrinkled as an old beige sheet. Seagulls and swans padded flat footed.

"Yeah, look. I didn't know whether you'd ever speak to me again, Ruby, but I got your number from the B&B you stayed at cause I felt bad after I saw you. I needed to explain a few things. I couldn't believe it when you turned up in St. Malo."

His voice suddenly went very faint, and I thought he'd gone. "Blake?"

"It's okay. I'm still here. Damn phone. Yeah, I need to explain the business with Viv."

"You don't need to explain, Blake. I...well, there were things I didn't say to you, like how proud I am of your success. I should have congratulated you, but—"

He gave a tiny hiss of laughter. "Yeah, it's a dream come true. But I do have to explain. You're a great girl, Ruby, and...well, what we had was special. But the thing is, Viv and I got married because she was pregnant. Only been married a couple of months, and she lost the baby."

"Oh, I'm sorry."

"Yeah, I was sorry too. We only got married because she was pregnant, and we were pressured by parents and stuff. And when I met you...yeah, okay, I knew I shouldn't— and I never have before. But I pursued you because I liked you. Do you understand what I mean?"

"Yes, I understand."

"Man, I should have explained all this before. And the thing Viv said about groupies? That was bad. You know it wasn't like that...." His voice wavered again and disappeared.

I stayed quiet, holding my breath, not knowing what to say, hoping he would come back.

And then his voice again, soft in my ear. "Ruby? The thing is, I'm ringing because I don't want you to have bad thoughts of me. Yeah, I look like a seedy old rock star now, but really, I'm still here, the Blake who serenaded you with 'Ruby Tuesday.' I've never really gone away." With a smile in his voice, he started singing. "Goodbye, Ruby Tuesday, who could hang a name on you when you change with every new day, still gonna miss you...."

Tears threatened, hot and salty, right at the back of my eyes, and yet my heart rose because I knew this was a big thing for Blake, a big thing for him to ring me like this and explain. I knew for sure now that he cared and that if he'd been single, who knows what might have happened between us. But he had a responsibility to Viv and couldn't go back on that. And the strange thing was, I felt free now. Free as a bird, as free as one of those pesky seagulls, and free to do what I knew I should have done weeks ago.

Chapter Eighteen

I'd been sitting on my bed for ages staring at my phone, plucking up the courage to send a text message. One little text message, and I was umming and aahing like an idiot and feeling as if it was the hardest thing I'd ever had to do. As if I was writing a book or something important like that, a bestseller that would rise rapidly up the charts, just as all of Blake's records seemed to be doing at the moment.

To make it even worse, I had several versions of the message planned out in my head.

Hi James, it's Ruby…just wondered if you wanted to meet for a drink sometime?

No!

Hi James, hope u okay. Do you fancy meeting for a chat?

No!

James, I miss you and want to see you now!

No, definitely no!

Rose had urged me again—and Mum at very regular

intervals — just that morning, when we'd had coffee together in a little café bar by the harbor, to text him, and now, after arriving home and thinking hard about it, I was still dithering.

The Pilgrims' first album, "Conquering the Long Hard Road" — which I thought was a pretty cool title — had just been released, and I had to say, from what I'd heard of it, it was pretty good. Not all the tracks were loud heavy metal, but some even disco oriented, and even a bit of country and pop. Blake's voice, when not in scream mode, was fab. Very reminiscent of his earlier guitar strumming acoustic days.

I'd taken to following the band on Facebook and Twitter, liking their pages and posting comments about how great their music was and congratulating them on their rise to stardom. I want Blake to know how much his phone call had meant to me and, as well as that, how it had allowed me to move on with my life. Well, that was if I could just do this one thing and be brave enough to send a text message to James.

I'd be far happier if *I* received a message *from* James but, what's that saying? "If the mountain won't go to Mohammed, then Mohammed will go to the mountain?" A bit of a weird quote, but I got the general gist, so yeah, I supposed that's what I was doing — or trying to do.

To everyone's surprise — except mine, I suppose, seeing as Rose had already given me the heads up — Rose and Steve were getting engaged, and a date had been set, and a party booked at the Coal Exchange to celebrate the occasion. Mum and Dad were thrilled, and as Leah had been invited too, she wanted to make sure she had the newest and best outfit and had been nagging at Daddy Michael to buy her one. I suppose the next couple to do the same would be Vanessa and Craig, but they'd not said anything yet, so that remained to be seen.

I'd never seen a man so changed as Michael since Leah came into his life. He even had an interview lined up at *The Emsworth Echo*, thanks to another of Dad's contacts. As much as he was enjoying his job at the pub, his enthusiasm for life, in general, had come back with a vengeance, and we could all tell that he was itching to get back to his old career as a reporter for a "local rag," as he called it.

So far, Priscilla has kept religiously to the visiting arrangements, and every time Michael arrived to pick her up, Leah was there, her little Mickey Mouse bag at her feet, ready and waiting at the door for Daddy. As well as cheering me up in my present miserable state, her presence in our lives seemed to have brought the whole family together. Mum was even closer to Nan and Grandad now, and any animosity she once had for them for advising her to give Michael up had totally disappeared. So, apart from my sad old story, everybody was happy.

Ah, I suddenly thought, looking around the bedroom with a keen eye. *At least when Rose moves out to be with Steve, this room will be mine, all mine. I can get a double bed, and the divider can go on the scrap heap.* I gazed around, making mental plans for the refurbishment, excitement coursing through me at the thought of a room of my own because, obviously, Rose and I wouldn't be buying a place together now.

A band of yellow sunshine streamed through the window, and, peering between the curtains, I saw that the black clouds from earlier had disappeared and the sun glowed in a blue sky speckled with fluffy tendrils of cloud. Deciding that I would go for a walk, I picked up my rucksack, automatically filling it with the things I would need — a water bottle, purse, keys, and lastly but most importantly, my phone. Just as I had picked it up and was putting it in my bag, it beeped, right there in my hand, jumping like a living thing in my palm.

Curiously I glanced at the screen to see the little text message icon flashing. Pressing the icon with a shaking finger, my heart beating hard and fast, I saw that at last, after all the waiting and wondering, it was from James. I read it eagerly, taking in all the words.

Hey Ruby, didn't like to get in touch sooner, but I have to know. Did you find what you were looking for in St. Malo? Jx

~*~

The whole world seemed muted and hazy as I stepped out of the empty house and walked down the garden path. Mum, Dad, and Rose must have gone out earlier without me realizing it. The garden was neat and tidy, baking under the spring heat, the earth in the borders dry and crumbly and the flowers drooping their heads.

The High Street was busy, so busy that I was worried I wouldn't be able to get through the crowds. What was going on? The sound of a brass band playing a rousing tune carried on the salty breeze, and as I walked nearer, I saw banners strung across the street, the words Happy St. George's Day written across them in thick black letters. Of course, it was April, already two months since I'd set off on my wild goose chase to France. Bunting of red, white, and blue fluttered merrily amongst the trees, and people, clapping, dancing, and waving flags, were gathered around an acoustic singer — a young man who, I saw with a pang, looked a bit like Blake —

and jugglers and stilt walkers paraded up and down the cobbles. Several young people were giving out programs of the activities for the day.

Fast food outlets were going a storm, long queues straggling across the road, and the smell of frying onions, burgers, and chips hung in the air. Definitely a recipe for every seagull's dream. Kids ran around with their faces painted like tigers and lions and dogs, as well as fairies, monsters, and even the distinctive red and white St. George's flag. Adults too! Leah would have loved it. Groups of students I recognized from school walked along in packs, glued to their phones.

I gave Mum and Dad a cheerful wave as I saw them going into the Coal Exchange with their friends Lenny and Sue, Dad rubbing his hands together in anticipation of the specialty pizza—and a beer or two with Michael, I'd no doubt. Then I caught an unexpected glimpse of Rose and Steve laughing companionably as they sat on the harbor wall licking giant ice-cream cones.

The sweet, cloying smell of incense weaved from the open door of the tarot shop, reminding me of the reading I'd had and what she'd said about me having to choose between two lovers. While I was glad to see that the shop was still flourishing—there were loads of people browsing inside— she hadn't really been that accurate with my reading...well, not the romantic side of it anyway. The prediction about my job had been spot on, but the choice between two lovers? No, that was a realization, not a choice.

A squealing microphone suddenly burst into a loud crackle, and the mayor of the local council, wearing the full regalia, took to the tiny makeshift stage and began to thank everybody for turning up to make St. George's Day so special. The crowd cheered wildly as he regaled them with funny stories, praised the lovely hot weather, and reminded them again of the exciting, fun-filled program for the day while waving one of the glossy brochures like a flag.

The band started up again with a jolly tune as I tried to push my way through the heaving throng, hot bodies barricading me from every angle. I battled against the oncoming tide of people, pushing and shoving until at last I was clear and, hurrying away, left the St. Georges festivities behind me. I carried on to Warblington, along the windy country lanes, past the eerie Pook Lane, where supposedly, ghosts of ethereal young ladies and lumbering black funeral carriages carrying tiny coffins had been seen by the locals — as well as the headless horseman, no doubt! Past the remains of Warblington Manor, just a tower spiraling up into the clouds, and so to St. Thomas a Becket Church, squatting low amidst the tombstones as a cat about to spring at a bird.

A large sign propped up against the old wrought iron cemetery gates beckoned me, and, moving closer, I saw that it read, Church open 12 noon till 4.00 p.m. in honor of St. Georges Day. Please come inside. The sun shone even brighter, and the intense heat was burning into the top of my head, so, curious and needing a breather, I slipped into the gaping black hole of the doorway, my eyes slowly adjusting to the dim as I went in.

The church was empty and quiet, the old musty smell strong. I breathed it in, reveling in how old this place was, the history, as I wandered around slipping silently amongst the tiny wooden benches admiring the ancient tiled floor, immaculately shiny in the sunlight that beamed in dusty shafts through the beautiful stained glass windows. Standing at the nave, I bowed my head to Jesus, who drooped so melancholy from a beautiful ornate cross.

Sitting on a bench quite alone, although who knows what ghosts and ghoulies hovered around me, I took my phone from my rucksack and once again read the text message I'd received from James. A text message that had made my heart pound with excitement and relief. And how strange it was that just as I had made up my mind to get in touch, he had beat me to it after all. It must be all the praying I'd done.

I read it again, realizing that, just as I hadn't dared to text him, he also hadn't dared to text me. It didn't look like his mum or Lara had told him about my visit to them because he obviously knew nothing of what had happened in St. Malo. I was surprised about that—I thought they would have gotten in touch straight away and relayed every word to him. It had taken a while, but I knew now what I wanted to say, so I scrolled to messages, my hands shaking as I tapped it out on the screen. *No, there was nothing in St. Malo. I've realized that everything I ever wanted, I'd left right here at home. Rx*

I waited then, for an answering beep, for a message to pop up on the screen, but there was nothing, and time went by, loud as a ticking clock in my head. Silently I rose to my feet and left the church, and walked out into the now blindingly hot sunshine and through the cemetery, stopping once again to read the heart-shaped stone for the little girl, Becky, and then wandering to James's dad's stone, where I saw that new flowers had recently been put. Lilies this time, sheaves of fragrant creamy white lilies.

I loitered for a few minutes, wondering if James would come here — he would probably guess that I would be out walking today and remember that we'd met here before on that snowy day a few months ago. But he didn't come. There was no tall figure, a beaming smile on his wide open face, walking towards me, arms outstretched for a hug. With an awful sinking feeling, I thought that maybe my text had put him off. Maybe his text had just been a friendly inquiry, and my answer had thrown him, embarrassed him even.

With a jolt, I realized that, because I hadn't been in touch, he might have assumed that my visit to St. Malo had been successful and Blake was now mine and that James had simply been trying to tie up loose ends with an old girlfriend before he moved on. Or maybe he had decided to take up the new contract in the Southampton branch of Sonic and was just wanting to say goodbye. That had never occurred to me before, even though his mum, Jacky, had said he'd been thinking about going for the new job.

Oh, James, I thought desperately. *Why won't you text?* Making me jump, my phone pulsed and lit up in my hand, where I'd been holding it tightly as if it was a lifeline. A text.

Ruby, we need to talk. I'm at the Royal Oak, can you get here soon?

Immediately I replied, *Yes, I'm on my way!*

I rushed then, as if pursued by the hounds of hell, out of the cemetery, past the monuments and the crosses and the massive family tombs. I set off across the fields, running past cows and sheep that, momentarily startled, lifted their great heads from their constant nuzzling of the grass. Pounding over the stony beach, slipping and stumbling on seaweed and shells, I reached the sleepy mill pond, the surface rippling with the fluttering of birds, droplets of water flashing iridescent in the sunshine. Breathless now and panting, I turned down past the Old Mill, its black tower shiny as licorice reaching for the sky, and the sea, shimmering in the sunshine, stretched to the horizon, scrubby reeds poking through the mirrored surface.

Chattering people sat outside The Royal Oak on benches or along the harbor wall, clutching drinks in sweaty hands, and the smell of fish and chips snaked from the open doorway. The sea lapped gentle as a sigh onto the stony beach. Wood pigeons cooed and swans, flat footed and ungainly, begging for scraps. My heart beating fast and squinting, shading my eyes from the sun. All I could see was the red outline of a tall figure walking slowly towards me. At last — was it really him? Was it really James?

He pulled me into his arms, the flowers he held crushed between us, the cellophane wrapper crackling. The scent of pink and red carnations, sweet as sugar, exploded around me as James's stubbly cheek rasped against mine.

The flowers fluttered to the ground and languished at our feet as, holding me at arm's length, a worried look in his deep brown eyes, he asked, "Was it me that you realized you'd left at home?"

I nodded, my throat too full of tears to speak. I was aware that people were looking at us, outright stares and covert glances. Kids were giggling and making mou mou kissing sounds.

Gathering me close again, he whispered into my ear. "I love you, Ruby. Always have, always will, ever since we were kids."

The realization that James still loved me finally broke the dam, and I burst into noisy sobs, hot salty tears streaming down my cheeks and my neck, soaking into James's skin and trickling into his T-shirt. Our faces slid wetly against each other, and, giggling like children, I stood on my tiptoes and whispered into his ear, "I love you too."

"That's all I ever wanted to hear," he whispered back. Clinging tight, James's body curving around mine, he cupped the back of my head in his palm until finally, our lips met in a kiss that sent shivers running down my spine. Yes! I'd finally come home.

To our surprise, the crowd rose to its feet and cheered heartily, everybody teary-eyed, waving their arms in the air. James did a sweeping courtier's bow and I a dip of a curtsy, and everybody cheered some more. And then, laying the flowers carefully as a baby in my arms, he clasped my hand in his and led me into the pub.

"You won't run away from me again, will you, Ruby?"

"No, never," I told him, shaking my head and thinking how warm and comforting his hand felt clasping mine. The tiny sandy beaches of St. Malo and the infatuated girl who was Ruby Tuesday wandered fleetingly as a ghost through my mind. I thought of the dark corners in La Bar, and the strains of Blake's voice echoed eerily in my head, but really I knew, without a doubt, that this was where I was meant to be. Right here with James.

"We've got a lot to talk about," he said as we sat down at a table by the window with our drinks. The bar was dim and cool after the heat outside, and bands of yellow sunlight fell through the windows onto the stone-flagged floor. The fireplace was clean and swept, a large vase of dried flowers in place of the fire that had roared up the chimney on that snowy day only a few months ago.

"Yes, we have," I replied. The sweet scent of the carnations wreathed around us as, leaning very close to him, I said, "But do you know what, James? First things first. I want to know when you're going to kiss me some more — especially the way you did just now."

His mega-watt magical smile was the only answer I needed.

THE END

About the Author

Debbie Chase (married name Debbie Spink) was born in Emsworth in Hampshire in 1959, although she has lived in West Yorkshire since 1979. She is the eldest of five children (two sisters and two brothers) and has many nieces and nephews, great-nieces and nephews, aunties, uncles and cousins, having come from a very large family. She has been married since 1984 and has one daughter, Lara, and three cats Ruby, Teddy and Maurice.

She has always been a reader and has enjoyed writing since school. Her proudest moment being when she achieved an A+ for an essay! She has had many short stories and poems for adults and children published in books and magazines. She has written four other books, the first being part fact/part fiction and called "You to Me Are Everything." The second book based on a real-life pet sitting job is called "The Confessions of a Pet Sitter (from the Pet's Point of View), and the third, the sequel to that book, "What a Catastrophe (Teddy's Tale). The fourth book is a book of poems called "I Wasn't There." All four books are available to buy on Amazon and many other online book stores as a paperback or kindle. She has also had two pocket novels ("Planning on Love" and "Romance on the Run") published with My Weekly magazine. Another pocket novel "Puppy Love" will be published with My Weekly in April 2021. Her other novels, "Educating Maggie" and "A Step Back in Time" are published right here with World Castle Publishing, with another "Ruby Tuesday" coming out soon.

Her other hobbies are Dance Inc workouts, walking, yoga, running, kettlebell workouts and Pilates.

After many years of office work, pub work and shop work, she is now partially retired and works part-time as an Examination Invigilator in a local school and also volunteers in a Cat's Protection charity shop.

Visit her website: https://www.debbiechase.rocks/

www.ingramcontent.com/pod-product-compliance
Lightning Source LLC
Chambersburg PA
CBHW030336180626
46810CB00003B/1376